THE WHOLE, ENTIRE, COMPLETE TRUTH

For Mike, Natasha, and Jacob Pattison,
who spend a lot of time without me
so that I can write.

The Whole, Entire, Complete Truth

Caroline Rennie Pattison

A BOARDWALK BOOK
A MEMBER OF THE DUNDURN GROUP
TORONTO

Editor: Barry Jowett
Copy-Editor: Andrea Waters
Design: Jennifer Scott
Printer: Webcom

National Library of Canada Cataloguing in Publication Data

Pattison, Caroline Rennie
The whole, entire, complete truth / Caroline Rennie Pattison.

ISBN-10: 1-55002-583-X
ISBN-13: 978-1-55002-583-5

I. Title.

PS8631.A84W46 2005 jC813'.6 C2005-903980-9

1 2 3 4 5 10 09 08 07 06

Conseil des Arts du Canada
Canada Council for the Arts
Canada

We acknowledge the support of the **Canada Council for the Arts** and the **Ontario Arts Council** for our publishing program. We also acknowledge the financial support of the **Government of Canada** through the **Book Publishing Industry Development Program** and **The Association for the Export of Canadian Books**, and the **Government of Ontario** through the **Ontario Book Publishers Tax Credit** program, and the **Ontario Media Development Corporation.**

Care has been taken to trace the ownership of copyright material used in this book. The author and the publisher welcome any information enabling them to rectify any references or credit in subsequent editions.

J. Kirk Howard, President

Printed and bound in Canada.
Printed on recycled paper.

www.dundurn.com

Dundurn Press
3 Church Street, Suite 500
Toronto, Ontario, Canada
M5E 1M2

Gazelle Book Services Limited
White Cross Mills
Hightown, Lancaster, England
LA1 4X5

Dundurn Press
2250 Military Road
Tonawanda, NY
U.S.A. 14150

for
My Dad
by
Sarah Martin

You wanted to know how I got mixed up in your investigation, Dad, and how I got Roy and Mindi involved, so here it is. In black and white, exactly like you ordered at the police station ... a detailed recounting of everything *that led up to the night when* everything *went wrong. Just like a real detective's report.*

As you read this, please remember you wanted *to know all this stuff and I've already served my time by writing it. So, please don't get angry with me all over again. I did just what you asked: I wrote about* everything.

(So if you find it a bit boring at times, don't blame me! My life's not that exciting.)

The Beginning

Date: Thursday, August 30

Location: Somewhere Deep in the Muskoka Sticks

"We couldn't have moved out further into the boonies if we tried!" I scowled, my bike trailing behind my brother's.

Roy pulled his bike up into a wheelie, showing off as usual. "Stop complaining, Sarah. You haven't even given this place a chance. You just have to learn to make your own fun!"

I rolled my eyes. "Yeah, right, this is fun — biking with you."

I was miserable. Living in the country was even worse than I had imagined. No matter where you looked, there were trees and rocks and more trees and rocks. I didn't even *know* where the nearest mall was. Make our own fun? What a laugh. I couldn't even relax and ride my bike. There were so many potholes and pebbles on our rundown road, I had to concentrate just to keep my balance.

The sun was getting low in the sky, darkening the woods on either side of us. There were no street lights to turn on and light our way. It felt a bit creepy. We'd only lived here a couple of weeks and I wasn't used to country living yet. The city streets were still my familiar territory. My eyes darted back and forth from the road to the forest.

"You know, Roy ..." I yelled up at him.

"Yo!"

"There could be anything in this bush, watching us."

"Don't try to freak me out, Sarah, it won't work," was his reply.

"I'm serious," I protested. "Just think about it. What would we do if a moose or some other animal hiding back in there suddenly charged us? Let's face it, we're helpless out here, all alone. Sitting ducks."

"You mean biking ducks." Roy snorted. He slowed down a little, and I caught up to him.

"Is big brave Sarah getting scared?" he asked me with mock concern. He did that funny thing with his eyebrows, making them go up and down really fast. What a goof. "Do you want your big strong brother to protect you from the scary wild animals?"

"As if." I gave him my best glare. "I'm not scared. I just think it's pretty dark in those trees. You can't see a thing in there. Anybody ... or anything ... could be in there watching us, right this minute, and we'd never know it — unless *they* wanted us to."

Roy's eyes grew to the size of golf balls. He let go of his handlebars and put his hands to his face, framing his gaping mouth.

"You're right, Sarah. I think I see something now! Oh my *gosh*! It's a big, scary raccoon! Pedal for your life! *Aaaaaahhhh*!"

Roy pumped the pedals of his bike hard and careened down the road at top speed, leaving me far behind, surrounded by the ever darkening woods. I watched him go. Trust Roy to leave me all alone in this hostile country environment. To my disgust, I wasn't kidding about being nervous. Give me the city streets anytime over trees. Besides, I heard raccoons can be ferocious. No kidding. I went back from looking at the road under my wheels to looking at the trees on either side of me, absently wishing I didn't have an idiot for a brother.

"Hey! There's a house up here, Sarah!" yelled Roy. He stopped his bike and cupped his hands to his mouth. Looking skywards, he announced, "Houston! We have signs of civilization."

I smiled in spite of myself and picked up speed. Another house, finally. This I had to see. I stopped beside Roy. Sure enough, set way back in the bush, quite a distance from the road, was an actual house!

From what we could see through the trees that lined the long driveway, it looked as though the house had seen better days. I'd like to say that it looked like the beautiful old-fashioned farmhouses you see on Christmas cards — minus the snow, of course — but I'd be lying. Truthfully, it looked like a strong wind could knock it over.

"There you go. We have neighbours after all. Are you happy now?" Roy asked.

"Yeah, gee whiz, neighbours you have to ride ten hours on a bike to get to," I said with a sniff. "It doesn't even look like anybody lives here."

"There's a mailbox."

Sure enough, there was. I examined it, feeling annoyed that Roy had noticed it before I had. I like to think of myself as the observant one. The detective. *Like you, Dad.* Unlike the house, the mailbox looked brand new. The gleaming wood had blue jays and sunflowers painted on it. It was pretty, in a Sticksville sort of way. The name *Braemarie* was displayed on the nameplate.

"Brand new mailbox, yucky old house," I commented.

Roy shrugged. "Ya gotta start somewhere."

I gazed through the trees. Maybe it was the spiffy mailbox or maybe it was just boredom, but for whatever reason, I had to get a closer look at that house. I wrestled my bike through the thick trees behind the mailbox and leaned it behind a particularly large one. My hope was that it would be hidden from the road.

"Sarah, what are you doing?" Roy asked.

"I'm going to get a closer look."

"A closer look? You can't do that. It's called trespassing. That's against the law. You could get arrested."

I crossed the driveway and started picking my way through the bush towards the house.

"Stop! C'mon, Sarah. You can't do this!"

He whined a whole lot more until finally I couldn't take it anymore.

"Roy, would you just shut up!" I whisper-yelled over my shoulder. "All I want to do is see the house up close. I'm not planning to rob the place or anything. How chicken are you, anyway?"

I kept walking. Roy doesn't realize it, but the more he tries to talk me out of something, the more I want to do it. He sighed and grunted as he hid his bike behind the mailbox with mine and caught up to me. Together we made our way through the trees towards the old house. It was the first excitement I'd had since being forced to move here. Pathetic? I know.

As we neared the house, we stayed in the cover of the trees and skirted around the driveway, which curved to the right. This led us to the far right of the farmhouse. Tall, thick, wild raspberry bushes bordered that side of the yard. I knew they were raspberry bushes because our house had them too. My mom had already threatened a family day of raspberry picking next summer. Yuck.

We crouched behind the raspberry bushes. The house was set in a huge clearing. It looked better close up, and there were obvious signs that renovations were going on. A brand new front porch was partially built; its wood looked raw and bright against the dull brown bricks of the house. The roof's new shingles were bright red. The house was a two-storey, like ours, and had a little rickety balcony coming off a door on the second floor.

I could hear faint whinnies and grunts coming from behind the house. Roy reluctantly followed me while, crouched over, I made my way along the raspberry bushes to get closer to those sounds. Two other buildings sat behind the house. The closer one was wooden and rectangular with two large doors that had been left propped open; the sounds came from inside. I'm not such a city slicker that I didn't recognize it as a horse stable. After all, I have seen pictures of such things. The second one was a large old barn. It was across the field from the stable, at the far edge of the clearing. Dirt tire tracks in the grass forked off the bend in the driveway and led up to it.

"This place is huge," I whispered.

Roy tugged at my arm. "Okay, you've seen the house up close now. Happy? It's a farmhouse. There's nothing special about it. We need to go home before it gets dark." He turned to go.

"Wait a minute," I whispered. "Someone's coming, get down."

We crouched down so low behind the bushes that our chins rested on the cool earth. I peeked through tiny gaps between the prickly branches in front of me and found I had a fairly decent view of the stable. I ignored Roy, who was practically having a heart attack right beside me.

A tall man with arms the size of tree trunks appeared at the stable doors. He was pushing a wheelbarrow piled high with the stinkiest, lumpiest stuff I'd ever smelled. A shovel had been stabbed into the heart of it.

Roy's face drained of colour as the man steered the wheelbarrow directly toward the raspberry bushes where we hid. My heart pounded so hard I was sure it was like a beacon, leading the man straight to us. Once he discovered us, he'd reach for his shovel and chase us off his property as if we were rabid dogs.

The big man grunted to a stop on his side of the raspberry bushes, but rather than chase us with his shovel, he simply threw it to the ground. Then he tilted up the arms of the wheelbarrow to dump out the stinky contents. Manure. He tossed it from side to side as it slid down and out of the wheelbarrow. It flew everywhere, right through our bushy cover. We were pelted with bits of the smelly stuff, and at one point a huge chunk of it bounced right off Roy's left cheek.

When the wheelbarrow was empty, the man picked up the shovel and began spreading the manure and mixing it into the soil. Roy and I stayed as still as statues. I'm pretty sure we weren't even breathing. All that man had to do was go up on his tiptoes, lean over just a little bit, and peek over the top of those bushes and he'd see us — crouched on our hands and knees, spotted all over with chunks of things previously digested by animals. Talk about scary — and disgusting.

Finally he was done. He turned his wheelbarrow and headed back toward the stable. We weren't discovered after all. I pried my fingers off Roy's arm and started to breathe again.

"When we get out of here, I'm going to kill you," croaked Roy, wiping his face. Apparently, that piece of manure hadn't bounced off his cheek as I thought; it had stuck there. Dirt attracts dirt, I guess. I couldn't help it; I pressed my smelly hands over my mouth to smother hysterical giggles.

"Shhh! He's back," said Roy. He bit down on his lower lip, turning it white. I stopped giggling.

We peered once again through the gaps between branches. The man was standing in front of the open stable doors. He checked his watch and tilted his head skywards then cupped his large hands to his mouth.

"Mindi!" he bellowed into the darkening air. The silence afterward was deafening; even the crickets were stilled. I held my breath, afraid to make a sound. Finally, a slight figure on horseback emerged from a trail in the woods to the left of a large fenced field.

"Coming, Colin," called a girl's voice. The crickets resumed their chirping. I began to breathe again.

The man stood with his arms crossed and watched her swift approach. I felt Roy's hand squeeze my shoulder as the horse trotted towards the waiting man. The girl's bronze hair bounced in time to the horse's gait.

"Hold on there, Mindi," the man ordered when it appeared that she was going to trot right by him and head straight into the stable. His voice was deep and authoritative. With a slight frown, the girl pulled her horse to a stop.

"I thought our deal for today was that you could ride the horses after you cleaned the stalls," he said, arms still crossed.

Mindi's eyes widened slightly. "Oh, I forgot … well, I can do it now …."

"Don't bother. I've already done it," he sighed. He looked toward the house and frowned.

"Sorry, Colin. I just thought I should exercise Candy before it got too dark."

"And that would normally work, but as I told you earlier, I'm expecting business guests tonight. You and your mother need to head home before they get here, and now you've made everything run late." The man scowled and scratched his short blond hair. "Let's go. Your mother's waiting for you." He jerked his head towards the house.

She jumped down from the horse and together they walked toward the stable doors, Mindi leading the horse.

"You haven't also forgotten that the old barn is out of bounds, have you?" asked the man.

"No, I never go near the barn," was her earnest reply.

Their voices faded as they entered the stable. Roy and I were alone once again.

"C'mon, let's get out of here!" Roy whispered. He grabbed my hand and pulled me all the way back to our bikes.

I didn't want to leave. I wanted to keep listening to Mindi and Colin talk. I felt as though I had been watching a play and only the first scene was over. I had to see more.

On our bikes once again, Roy sped home without a backward glance. I, on the other hand, couldn't stop looking.

So, Dad, now you know how it all began. It was very innocent, wouldn't you say? How were we to know that a simple bike ride one evening would eventually land us at the police station? Who could know that Mindi was destined to become my closest friend?

THE DAY I MET MINDI

DATE: TUESDAY, SEPTEMBER 4

LOCATION: SCHOOL

My first day of school was awful. I had been looking forward to starting high school in Mississauga with my friends. It was going to be exciting. Instead, I was here, all alone, in Sticksville. Totally not-exciting. Not to mention that I'm at a critical age when social acceptance and healthy peer group belonging are the major determinants for positive life choices and development. (I read that in a magazine.) What kind of parents would drag their perfectly happy child away from her life and her friends and force her to go to a brand new school among strangers at this critical time in her life?

Oh yeah … mine.

First impressions? Not good. The high school in our little town was tiny by Mississauga standards. And the kids! I'd never had so many people staring at me and whispering in my entire life. It was even worse than when I had toilet paper stuck to my shoe for an entire song during my grade eight graduation dance! I was either a celebrity or a freak show to them, I couldn't tell. I figured it must be pretty boring here in Sticksville if a new kid at school could cause such a stir.

Things started looking up a little when I discovered that Mindi, the girl on horseback, was in my homeroom class. At least it was a familiar face — to me, that is. It wasn't as if I had an instant pal or anything. And she definitely wasn't in the market for new friends, like I was. In fact, as I walked into homeroom that first morning, she was giggling with a couple of girls at the back of the room. I felt a stab of envy; in Mississauga, I would be giggling with friends, too.

Sad to say but the highlight of my day — which, by the way, turned out to also be the only time someone actually talked to me — was this stupid icebreaker game that the teacher made us play. You know, the kind that's supposed to make everybody feel warm and cozy. The class was paired up and we interviewed each other. Then we introduced our partners to the rest of the students, describing all we had learned. Talk about putting new students through torture on their first day of school.

I was paired up with one of Mindi's giggling girlfriends. Her name was Cori Stedman. She looked like the type of girl who thought she had the world wrapped up with her cute face and bouncy hair. We moved our chairs so that we could sit across from each other. With a toss of her head, Cori swung her golden locks back over her shoulder and sat poised with her pen and paper. She looked annoyed at being stuck with the new person, and she kept glancing wistfully over at her friends.

"Okay, let's get this over with," she said with a sigh. She didn't even look up from her paper. I could've been sitting there naked for all she knew. "I'll interview you first. What's your name?"

I was getting irritated — I mean really, was that any way to welcome the new kid? So since it was obvious she couldn't care less about getting to know me, I gave her the full, unabridged answer. No holds barred.

Taking a deep breath, I said, "My name is Sarah Martin. I lived in Mississauga until my parents dragged me up here without ever asking me if I wanted to move ... which I didn't. I used to live in a big new house where I could hang out my bedroom window and practically touch the house next door, and now I live in this big old house with no neighbours in sight that's out of town as far as you can get a bus to go from this rinky-dink school. Maybe you know it, it's Bill Brown's old house — at least that's what they call it in town. I have no idea when it'll be considered *our* old house." Cori was actually looking at me now so, encouraged, I kept going. "Anyway, I have a brother in grade ten who is a total pain in the butt. We live with both our parents ... no, they're not divorced, although they do fight once in a while. My dad's an OPP detective. He was sick of living in a busy city, so he asked for a transfer, which is why we ended up here. It didn't seem to matter what the rest of us wanted to do. My mom doesn't have a job here yet, but she used to work in a dentist's office.

"I don't have any pets, although since we moved to Sticksville my mom has been talking about getting some pigs — I guess she's bored with no job. She used to keep pretty busy. I don't know why she'd want to get pigs, though. Like, what would she know about pigs? Nothing! Unless you count the pig in *Charlotte's Web*. She knows a lot about him because she read the book to me when I was in grade two." I stopped to take a breath. Let's see Miss Perfect get all that down on paper!

Cori was staring at me as if I was some kind of mutant insect, pen still raised. She hadn't moved. She hadn't written a thing. What kind of reporter was she?

I smiled sweetly at her.

"Anything else you'd like to know?" I asked, feigning politeness.

"Does everybody from Mississippi talk as much as you?" she asked, with a scowl.

"Mississauga," I corrected her.

"Whatever."

As you can see, we hit it off.

Eventually, I had to stand up in front of the class so everyone could stare some more while Cori reported her findings. She actually told them only a fraction of what I had told her and she got most of it wrong. Memory obviously wasn't her strong point. She should have written something down. Well, now at least they all had a name for me. That, she got right.

I felt like repaying her poor memory by making up some tidbits about her that I'm sure the class would find interesting but I thought that would be pushing things a little too far. After all, I wasn't in the business of making enemies. So I behaved myself and told the class exactly what she told me. I have a good memory for trivial information — and believe me, this was very trivial: basically, she lived in town and she liked playing basketball and watching TV. Thrilling, eh?

From Mindi's partner, I learned that Mindi lived in town, close to the school and close to her friend Stacey. She loved horses, basketball, and summer holidays. Her best friends were Cori and Stacey.

That pretty much sums up my only human contact all day, not counting the time I spent with the teacher, who chatted with me for about two minutes to make me feel welcome. You know how people say, "If only I could have been a fly on the wall?" Well, that's pretty much what I was that day. And believe me, it's not all it's cracked up to be.

By 3:30, I was actually looking forward to the never-ending bus ride home. I hurried to the back of the school where the buses wait for us "rural" kids. Roy was already there. He was talking and laughing with several other boys as I approached. I could tell right away that he was in show-off mode. That's never a good thing for me.

"Hey, Sarah!" he shouted.

Everyone heading for the buses turned and stared. Just what I needed after the day I'd had. More staring. But what could I do except put on my brightest smile as though it didn't bother me one bit that my brother was about to humiliate me in front of total strangers. I kept walking on stiffening legs, trying my best to look cool.

Roy threw an arm across my shoulders and steered me towards the boys he had been standing with.

"Let me introduce you to my new friends," he said, his loud voice causing yet more heads to turn. "Sarah, this is Kurt, Dave, Chris, and John. This is my sister, Sarah."

The boys were gaping at me with goofy grins. Morons. I shot Roy a look but he ignored me, wearing the same goofy grin as the others.

"I told you she looks a lot better since the plastic surgery," Roy announced proudly. "You can hardly see the hideous scars."

"Ugh! Loser!" I wheeled out from under his arm as Roy doubled over in laughter. My brother can be a real jerk. It was the perfect ending to a perfectly rotten day.

With their ridiculous cackling echoing in my ears, I boarded the bus and, to my surprise, spied Mindi sitting alone near the back. Probably going back to that farmhouse, I guessed. I was heading towards an empty seat when another explosion of laughter from Roy and his new friends burned into my brain. How could I sit by myself and let Roy see how I couldn't make a single friend all day? Determined not to be a total loser, I passed the empty seat and headed straight for Mindi, hoping that she wasn't saving the seat beside her for someone.

"Hi," I said, pasting on a cheerful face.

"Hi," she answered, looking mildly surprised.

"Do you mind if I sit here?" I asked.

"Sure," she shrugged, moving her knapsack to the floor between her feet to make room for me. I plunked myself down.

We sat in awkward silence for a few minutes. I started to wish that I'd just sat by myself.

"So, what made your family move to Muskoka?" asked Mindi, finally.

The dam opened. I told her all about our move

and how it tore out my guts to be taken from my friends. I put in lots of drama to make it more interesting. I wanted to be sure to hold her attention. So what if I had to embellish the facts a little for interest's sake?

I was really on a roll getting into my "woe is me" story when I realized, to my delight, that Mindi actually looked interested. Especially when I told her about my mom's insane desire to suddenly own farm animals — pigs, no less.

"Do you own any horses?" she asked.

"No, we don't actually have any animals yet."

"Oh ..." Mindi turned to look out the window, obviously disappointed.

"But I've always wanted a horse," I added, knowing that Mindi was a horse lover. "They're so beautiful." She turned back from the window and smiled at me.

"Yes, they are," she agreed. "So where exactly do you live, Sarah?"

I told her. Her face brightened.

"I go to my mom's boyfriend's farm just up the road from you. Maybe you could come over sometime and see his horses. It would be great to have someone else to ride with once in a while."

I could scarcely believe my ears. "Yeah, sure. That sounds fun," I told her, trying not to sound too excited. "I don't exactly know a lot about horses, though."

"That's okay, I can teach you. You'll love them!" said Mindi. She smiled at me. It felt so good to have someone finally smile at me. I felt like I had actually made a friend. I didn't have to go home a total friendless loner.

"Sounds great," I said, grinning.

"I usually go to Colin's, that's my mom's boyfriend, about two or three times a week after school. I clean out the horses' stalls, bring them in from the fields for the night, and feed them. Then they need to be exercised, so I get to ride them around all I want. There are lots of cool trails at the farm. You'd really like it."

"I can help you clean the stalls if you want," I offered.

"Really? That would be great. We can get out on the horses faster that way. Colin's been bugging me to get them done before I take the horses out."

I bit my tongue, realizing I'd almost said, "I know."

"It would be nice having someone else around," continued Mindi. "It gets a little boring doing everything by myself all the time. Colin and Mom don't always come out to the stable with me. My mom's an artist, she paints, so she likes to go over to the farm because she likes the atmosphere. She says it makes her feel more creative."

"Wow, an artistic mom," I said. "My mom's idea of being artistic is to use butter instead of margarine when she's cooking."

Then it was Mindi's stop. I waved to her from the bus and suddenly I realized my day was much brighter than it had been just half an hour ago. After the lousy day I'd had, who would have thought things could turn out so … promising?

As if it isn't bad enough that I have to write this huge report for you, Dad, I also have to have a know-it-all brother who demands to read everything I write. He says that I need to have a fact-checker, but really he wants to make sure I don't write anything that'll get him into trouble. So, he's insisting that he needs to approve everything I write before I give it to you. You see what I have to put up with?

Then last night I had to listen to Roy whine on and on about how I'm always putting him down in this report. I only write the truth. Honestly. He is *always showing off and acting like a goof. I can't help it if the truth hurts. Maybe he should learn something about himself. I told him to get a counsellor. He told me he was going to sue me for slander.*

Can he do that, Dad?

Mindi was surprised to read how nasty Cori was to me the first time we met — or should I say, Little Miss Perfect! Mindi felt really bad about it, but it had nothing to do with her. Cori and I are never going to be friends, there's nothing she can do about it.

Not only did I meet Mindi and Cori that first day of school, I also found out some things that made me wonder what was going on at the farmhouse where Roy and I first saw Mindi. And guess what, Dad? It was because of you *that I became suspicious of Mr. Braemarie in the first place. You provided the first real clue that things were not quite right.*

Dad's Clue

Date: Tuesday, September 4 (continued)

Location: Home and the Farmhouse

At suppertime on that first day of school I sat at the table and suffered through Roy's long-winded monologue about his *perfect* day and his *perfect* new friends. It was really something. That mouth of his just never stopped moving. He just kept yakking and yakking. How he managed to eat his supper and talk so much at the same time was beyond me. What a pig! No wonder Mom wanted one so badly: they remind her of her dear son.

I guess I shouldn't complain, at least one of us had something to talk about. I had finished eating and was tapping my fingers waiting to ask to be excused when Mom put a hand on my arm.

"How was your first day at school, dear?" she asked.

Oh great! Everyone looked at me, waiting for my answer. I had been hoping that they would just forget about me while getting the earful about Roy's *perfect* day.

"It was … okay," I answered, with a shrug.

"Did you meet any of the other kids?" she probed mercilessly.

My eyes shifted to Roy, who looked miffed at the loss of attention. The last thing I wanted was for him to know what a lousy day I had. So I told a tiny white lie.

"Well, I met Mindi and Cori in my homeroom class today. They're really nice." I felt my face heat up the way it does when I don't tell the whole truth. Not that I lie all the time or anything. I mean, some of this was true. I did meet both of them and *one* of them was nice to me. The other? Well, I didn't need to go into that.

"That's terrific, honey," said Mom. Dad smiled. They waited — obviously wanting me to go on. So I did.

"Mindi sometimes takes the same bus as me," I said, "when she goes to her mom's boyfriend's farm down the road after school, that is." Roy tried to catch my eye, but I ignored him. "She helps take care of his horses and she's allowed to ride them too. She told me that there's lots of trails to use and that if I want, she'd teach me stuff about horses and how to ride them."

My dad's expression changed as I spoke. His smile slowly turned into a frown.

"Which farmhouse are you talking about?" he asked.

"Just down that way." I pointed in the direction of the farmhouse. "The bus stop just before our house."

Dad didn't say anything. He just kept looking at me with that frown on his face.

I told him more. "It has a long driveway and looks like it's falling apart but I think it's getting fixed up. Anyway, it's our closest neighbour. C'mon, you know which one I mean."

He kept looking at me with that funny expression I couldn't quite read.

"Isn't that great, Dad?" I prompted. "I mean about Mindi saying that maybe sometime I could go over there? Imagine me on a horse! That would be so cool, don't you think?" I shifted in my seat. He still wore that weird face. Why wasn't he saying anything?

"Dad?" I asked. "What's wrong?"

His frown deepened. He cleared his throat. "I feel a little uneasy about you going over to a strange household with people I don't know. I think you need to hold off going over there until I get to know the man who actually lives in the farmhouse. I'll stop in and introduce myself."

I was dumbfounded. What was this about? I didn't hear him trying to screen the families of Roy's new friends. So why mine?

"When are you going to do that?" I asked, my heart sinking.

"I don't know exactly, I'm really busy at work right now. I'll get over there as soon as I can." He picked up his fork and pierced a piece of chicken.

Now I was angry. I made one lousy friend at school and my dad was giving me a hard time about it. This was injustice.

"So I have to wait — for how long?" I pressed.

"I'll get there as soon as I can," he said around a mouthful of food.

"What about Roy's new friends? When are you going to meet their parents?"

"I don't know."

This really made me lose it. I admit, I had a bit of a meltdown.

"I get it!" I shouted. "I'm not supposed to have any friends, but Roy can have as many as he likes. Don't you think you'd better meet Chris's dad? He might be an axe murderer! All I want to do is visit Mindi and see the horses. I don't care about her mother's boyfriend."

Dad slammed down his fork. "I *do* care about him!" he yelled. "It's his home you'll be going to. I have no idea who he is. A single man entertaining two young girls."

I stood up and my chair fell over behind me. "Dad!"

"Well? You never know."

"I don't believe this." *Her mom would be there!* "This is just stupid!"

"Watch it, Sarah." Dad's face turned to stone, a sure sign that I should stop. I couldn't.

"Well, how am I supposed to get to know someone if I can't even spend time with her when I'm invited to?" I argued, blinking back angry tears.

"You'll see her at school or you can have her over here," he stated firmly. "Now, sit down or leave the table." He picked up his fork and resumed eating. As far as he was concerned, the conversation was over.

I picked up my chair and sat down, silently appealing to my mom. She looked confused.

"Ed, don't you think you're being a little overprotective here? There are going to be new people in all of our lives. We can't know everything about them all right away. It would be good for Sarah to be around horses. Maybe it will help her appreciate the country more."

Dad sighed. "Gina, I just think we should know a little more about the person whose home Sarah is planning to spend time at," he stated matter-of-factly, as if he wasn't ruining my life in one sweeping statement. "You know as well as I do that our daughter doesn't always make the best decisions, and her going to a strange man's home makes me a little uneasy." Then he shot my mom one of those meaningful looks that meant they were having one of their silent conversations. This was usually not good for me.

"You're right, Ed," Mom finally agreed in a quiet voice. I think she still looked a little confused, though. "We don't know anything about Mindi or her mother's boyfriend. You're right to be cautious." She looked down at her food.

I stood up from the table and stamped my foot. Yes, I know it sounds childish but I was really angry. I couldn't help it.

"I don't believe this!" I shouted. "Roy sits here and tells you all about his new friends and everything's great." I clasped my hands together and did a cruel, but accurate, imitation of my parents. "*Ooooh, isn't Roy wonderful? Listen to all the great new friends he's made.* Well, I had a terrible day, thanks for asking. I only met two people and one of them doesn't even like me! Then, when I tell you about the one who does, I'm not even allowed to visit her without you doing a stupid police check! And she's the only person that's even close enough for me to visit after school. In case you haven't noticed, you stuck us out in the middle of nowhere here and I have no friends! You made me move away from all of them. Doesn't anyone around here want me to be happy? I hate this house!"

I stomped out of the kitchen.

"Sarah!" my mom called.

"Let her be," I heard Dad say. "She'll be fine."

What does he know? I thought, as I slammed shut the door of my bedroom.

After supper, my parents went out for their nightly walk, one of their new routines since our move here. I was still lying on my bed fuming when Roy started yelling at me to come down and help with the dishes. I ignored him, but he kept calling me. It was annoying, to say the least. Finally, I hoisted myself reluctantly off my bed.

"I'm coming!" I shouted, louder than needed. "Keep your pants on!"

As I passed the open door of Dad's office, I took a detour inside. I'm not sure why I did — it wasn't something I planned to do. I guess I was just prolonging the moment I had to share a room with *perfect* Roy. Anyway, there, on the large desk, sat Dad's briefcase. As a rule, it was always kept shut and locked tight whenever Dad wasn't there, but for some reason, that night it was wide open, stuffed full of the files of Dad's ongoing cases.

Let's call it fate.

Now, Dad, you have to understand. To me, this was simply irresistible. I'll admit, I'm probably one of the nosiest people on this planet. And although I do know that your briefcase is strictly off limits, at the time I was too mad at you to care. The sight of your open briefcase was just way too much of a temptation; you should have known better. My anger was immediately replaced by excitement. You know how much I love to hear about your detective work, and here was a golden opportunity to see actual files of your cases! Forbidden gold! Sitting right in front of me. What harm would one little look do?

I bounded over to the desk and looked down at the files. With trembling fingers, I began thumbing through them. Not looking for anything in particular, just looking and enjoying the feel of them — so official! Suddenly, a file labelled "Braemarie" caught my eye. That name sounded vaguely familiar. I wondered where I had heard it before. I was about to pull the file out to look inside when I heard Roy thumping up the stairs.

"Sarah! Quit being such a baby and get down here and help me with the dishes!" he bellowed.

I sprang away from the briefcase just as Roy stormed by the room.

"Hey!" He spun around and stopped in the doorway. "There you are," he said. "What are you doing in here?" Roy's eyes took in my hot, reddened face and the open briefcase. It was like a light went on in his head. He raised his hands in protest. "No way. You can't look in there, Sarah. Those are confidential police files!" he sputtered, echoing the warning that we had been given repeatedly over the years. Under no circumstances were we ever to meddle with the work Dad brought home. And up until that night, none of us had ever dared to.

Honestly, Dad.

"I know, Roy." I dismissed him with a wave of my hand. "I didn't actually look in any of the files. Relax. Does the name 'Braemarie' mean anything to you?"

"Sarah! I don't believe you. Just come downstairs."

"I will, I will. Just think for a minute, would ya? I know I've heard that name before," I coaxed.

He sighed. "Okay. Braemarie." He thought for a moment. "It does sound kinda familiar … wasn't it the name on that old farm's mailbox?"

Talk about a light snapping on. I should have recognized that name right away!

"Holy cow!" I said. "You're right! How could I be so stupid?"

"That's what I wonder all the time," Roy said. I ignored him.

"That name is on one of Dad's files!" I pointed to the briefcase.

"It's on one of Dad's files?" he repeated with a frown. "You mean that guy's being investigated?" Sudden understanding dawned on his face. "So that's why Dad made such a big deal out of you going over there."

"You catch on quickly, Sherlock."

Roy and I stared at each other. Wordlessly, we both grabbed for the open briefcase. Roy was a split second quicker than I was. He elbowed me roughly out of the way and had the briefcase shut and locked in seconds flat, ignoring my protests.

"Don't mess around with Dad's stuff!" he warned. "It'll only get you into trouble!"

"Trouble!" I yelled back at him. "I have a right to know what's going on since Dad won't even let me go over there. Now I'll never be able to look at the file — because of you! You're such an idiot!"

Roy stood firm, his face set. "I had to stop you, Sarah. If there *is* something going on with Mr. Braemarie —"

"There must be! Why else —"

"— the police will handle it, not you," he finished.

We stood there glaring at each other. Finally, I stomped out of the room.

"Whatever!" I yelled back at Roy in frustration. "Now I'll just have to find out what's going on there myself!" I ran down the stairs two at a time and stormed out the front door, slamming it as hard as I could behind me. I could hear Roy calling for me to come back, but nothing was going to stop me.

I jumped on my bike and pedalled madly down the driveway. My parents were in the distance returning home from their walk, but I pretended not to see them. I was too mad to care about them right then.

Dad, you should have just told me that there was something fishy about Mr. Braemarie. Instead, you kept it a big secret so that I had to go find out for myself. The hard way.

Once again, I found myself riding down our lonely country road casting uneasy glances into the darkening woods. A small part of me missed Roy's presence — a very small part. A bigger part still seethed at his I-know-what's-best attitude. Who did he think he was, anyway? And who did my parents think they were? They made me move up here to no man's land and then wouldn't even let me spend time with a new friend. The only one I was able to make!

Soon I could see the farmhouse, set back from the road, nestled comfortably among the trees. Right away, I checked the mailbox. Sure enough, the name on it was Braemarie. So Roy was right. Why did my father have a file on this guy? I had to find out, especially if it meant that Mindi was in danger. Maybe this guy was a psychotic serial killer! I gave my head a shake. I could practically hear Roy telling me I was getting carried away, as usual. Still, Mr. Braemarie must be doing *something* wrong. Police don't carry files on law-abiding citizens.

If Roy had really wanted me to mind my own business, he should have let me read that file. Then I wouldn't have had to try to figure out what was going on myself. You'd think he'd know how my mind works by now.

I stashed my bike in the trees behind the shiny mailbox so that it would be hidden from the road. I followed the driveway under cover of the thick forest that ran parallel to it. This led me towards the opposite side of the house from the approach Roy and I took the other day. I figured I'd get a better view of the entire area from this angle. As I got closer, the driveway veered off to the right, leading towards the front of the farmhouse, and a dirt trail forked to the left, leading towards the old barn. The one that Mr. Braemarie said was out of bounds to Mindi!

The house was dark and looked empty. However, there was a sleek black car on the trail leading up to the barn. A dim light shone from a small, high window. I decided to investigate. I was on the move, dodging around trees, heading towards the barn, thoroughly enjoying myself for the first time that day, when the barn door swung open and voices floated through the air towards me. I froze.

Emerging from the barn was the muscular, manure-shovelling man who I now knew was Colin Braemarie. He was accompanied by two other men, looking out of place in their dark, tailored suits. Mr. Braemarie's cropped blond hair caught the last low rays of the sun, making it stand out in sharp contrast to the dark hair of his visitors. I could hear the low murmur of their voices, but I couldn't quite make out what they were saying. How frustrating.

Mr. Braemarie made some wild gestures with his arms that made him and one of the men break into gales of hearty laughter. He seemed to be directing most of his conversation to the laughing man, who was quite tall and lean. The third man was shorter than the other two but looked as if he could lift up a car with little effort. He stood slightly apart from the others, looking official with his legs firmly planted and his arms crossed. He reminded me of a drill sergeant I saw in a movie once.

The men shook hands and the visitors stepped into their car. I crouched behind a tree and held my breath as the headlights of the passing car swept by me. Mr. Braemarie stood and watched until they reached the road then turned back into the old barn, closing the door firmly behind him.

I stood with a sigh. My curiosity meter was hitting an all-time high. Who were these men who visited barns at night, in suits? Why was the barn out of bounds for Mindi? I had to know what was going on! I made my way carefully through the trees. Then, wanting to get closer, I burst out into the open and sprinted, coming to a halt, gasping — more with adrenaline than exertion — with my back against the barn's rough wooden wall. I inched my way along it, wishing there was a window to peek into, but the only windows were too high and out of reach. I needed to see what was inside! I pressed my ear against the wall. I could hear some muffled, unidentifiable sounds along with the low rumble of Mr. Braemarie's voice. I squeezed my eyes shut and concentrated, straining to make out what he was saying. Who was he talking to?

Suddenly, a hand grasped my shoulder and whirled me around. I started to scream but another hand clamped my mouth shut. I blinked in terror. I was so scared, it took me a full minute to realize that it was Roy's face I was blinking at. I punched him on the arm — hard — and he let go of me.

"What do you think you're doing? You just about gave me a heart attack!" I whispered, pushing him away.

"Me? What are *you* doing? Playing spy games? Turning into a peeping Tom?" he whispered back. "I came to bring you home. Mom and Dad are ticked that you took off and left me with all the dishes to clean up. I told them I'd look for you."

"I'll go home when I'm ready," I retorted, turning my back to him. "I don't need you to come and fetch me."

His voice grew softer. "Let's go home *now*. It's almost dark, and there's nothing going on here for you to see."

Reluctantly, I had to agree with him. The mysterious men had left and there was no way of seeing what Mr. Braemarie was doing in the barn. With a final glance back, I let Roy lead me through the dark to where our bicycles were stashed.

I told him about the men in suits, but all he said was, "You just can't leave anything alone, can you?"

On our bikes, I remained a sullen distance behind Roy so that I could mutter and curse in solitude while trying not to think about the lecture I knew would be waiting for me at home.

So you see, Dad, you were the one who raised my suspicions about Mr. Braemarie in the first place — if you'd just let me visit Mindi, I wouldn't have been spying on Mr. Braemarie. And you shouldn't be leaving your briefcase out and unlocked with me around! You should know better! You said yourself that I don't always make the best decisions.

My next clue that something strange was going on came directly from Mr. Braemarie himself.

Mr. Braemarie's Clue

Date: Wednesday, September 5

Location: School and on the Bus

The second day of school, I walked into homeroom determined that it would be a better day. Mindi and her two friends, Cori and Stacey, were standing by their desks, chatting and giggling. They looked up as I walked over.

"Hi, Mindi," I said, my voice bright and cheery. Who wouldn't want to be friends with someone like me?

"Hi," Mindi said with a wave before promptly turning back to her friends.

Well, what did I expect? One bus ride and instant best friends? I plunked into my seat feeling dejected. Loner-ville, here I go again.

Eventually, people did talk to me. Mindi included. But Cori and Stacey kept pulling her away from me. They weren't very friendly. Well, I guess Stacey wasn't so bad, but that Cori ... we're just too different, I guess. For instance, she thinks she's great and I don't.

* * *

At the end of the day, Mindi took the bus to the farm again, so we walked to the back of the school together. This was the highlight of my day. No kidding.

Thanks again, Dad, for making me move here. No need to bore you with the details.

Walking with Mindi, I chatted and laughed and tried my best to be witty, but to my dismay, as soon as we were on the bus, I ran out of things to say. After all, my life isn't that interesting. So we rode together on that bumpy bus in an awkward silence for a long while. I fidgeted in my seat — searching my mind desperately to think of something to talk about. After all, I was trying to show her how fun I was. The last thing I wanted was to be boring. I tapped my foot, played with my hangnail, tried not to think about my itchy nose, but I couldn't think of a thing to say.

Finally, Mindi spoke. I almost fainted with relief.

"I talked to Colin — my mother's boyfriend — about you coming over after school someday," she said, looking down at her hands.

"Oh yeah? What did he say?" I prompted, wondering how I was going to tell Mindi I wasn't allowed.

"Well, at first he seemed okay about it, you know, happy that I had someone close by to spend time with at his place. Then later on, when I was grooming Candy and cleaning the tack, he came out to the stable and told me to hold off on inviting you over. When I asked him why, he just said things were too busy for him right now, with some of the extra business he's doing, and he'd rather I didn't have any friends around for a while." Mindi frowned. "Not that I ever do have friends around. He was kind of weird about it. Sorry."

She looked up from her hands and shrugged. She really did look sorry.

I shrugged too, trying to hide my disappointment and, in a way, relief. "That's okay," I said.

"It's not okay. I really wanted you to come over. It's not fair."

While her indignation made me feel wanted, I also felt angrier than ever that now I had two adults stopping me from making a friend. My one and only friend.

"You could always come over to my house instead sometime," I suggested meekly.

Mindi nodded. "I'd only be able to stay for a little bit, though, then I'd have to get over to the farm to clean the horses' stalls. It's my job."

"That's better than nothing."

"True."

I knew that these were only words; Mindi wouldn't be coming over anytime soon. I got the impression that she was too in love with her horses to part with them for long.

A growing commotion behind us caught our attention. We craned our necks around to look back and who do you think we saw? You guessed it — Roy. My goofy brother. He was sitting amidst his usual fan club making everyone laugh. At that particular moment, he himself was laughing so hard he could hardly speak. A blessing for the rest of us, believe me.

"So, is that your brother over there?" Mindi asked. "Roy? Is that his name?"

"Yeah, that's him," I admitted reluctantly. "Please don't hold it against me. You know what they say about not being able to choose your family."

"He's cute," Mindi said, giggling.

I just about keeled over. She obviously didn't have good taste in boys.

During the rest of the drive home, Mindi was so busy making goo-goo eyes back at Roy that I was left to do most of the talking. By that time, my brain had thawed out of its deep freeze and I seemed to have far too much to say. I ended up babbling about the stupidest things. I started off by describing the huge, unfair lecture I received from my parents for not helping Roy do the dishes the night before. My topics went downhill from there. When I began listing the kinds of pajamas each member of my family wore to bed at night, I could have kicked myself. The more Mindi stole glances back at Roy, the more I was unable to stop talking. It probably didn't matter anyway; I'm pretty sure she wasn't even listening to me. Roy had her full attention.

Finally, the bus rounded the last bend before the Braemarie farmhouse. By that time, it was pure relief to stop my monologue about stupid dog food commercials. We said good-bye, and she hopped down from the bus with one last gaze back at my dumb brother.

Be prepared, you're going to get mad when you read this next part, Dad. It's about how I began visiting Mr. Braemarie's farm even though you told me not to. You know, I really thought you were just being unfair. Sure, I knew you had a police file on him, but I figured it was for something lame, like tax fraud. It wasn't as if I was worried at all about my safety or anything like that. After all, Mindi was safe enough over there, so why would I be any different?

By the way, you have no idea how hard life is for a first-year high-schooler who is trying her best to make at least one friend. I pretty much spent the whole first week of school by myself. I felt like such a loser.

I had to go!

My First Illegal Visit to the Farm

Date: Monday, September 10

Location: School and the Farmhouse

"Sarah, over here!" called Mindi.

I gave her a grateful smile as I entered the change room. There's nothing like having your name called out to make you feel like you belong. Stacey and Cori watched my approach. Cori was frowning, as usual. Too bad for her. Maybe her face will get stuck like that one day. I plopped my knapsack on the bench beside them.

"I'm glad you decided to come to the tryouts," Mindi said.

"What the heck," I said, with a shrug.

"Do you talk as much on the court as you do in an interview?" asked Cori with a smirk.

I couldn't help it, I blushed. I hate feeling my face grow all hot like that, but it happens. Mindi glared at Cori. Stacey giggled.

To my delight, I discovered that I could hold my own out on the basketball court even with the grade ten girls. (I mentally thanked Roy for all those times this past summer he forced me to play one-on-one in the driveway — not that I'd ever tell him that.) I even had fun; it felt good to be running up and down the court, doing the drills, shooting baskets. And the other girls talked to me. For the first time since I arrived, I started to think that it just might be possible to fit in at this school after all.

But don't get me wrong here, Dad, I was still mad at you for moving us away from home!

Mindi caught up to me in the hall when I was consulting my school map, trying to remember how to get to my next class. My second week of school and I still didn't know how to get around. It's a very confusing building.

"Great playing, Sarah," she said.

"Thanks."

"Hey, do you feel like meeting me at Colin's after school today? I'll introduce you to his horses," she said.

I'm sure my jaw dropped in surprise.

"I thought you weren't supposed to have anyone over?" I asked.

Mindi grinned and raised her eyebrows wickedly. "Today doesn't count because Colin's not going to be at home. My mom's going to be there to do some painting and she said you're welcome to help me in the stable. So what do you think? Do you want to?"

Okay, honestly, Dad, I did have to think here — for about two seconds. I knew that you didn't want me to go there. So I really was in a bit of a dilemma; however, I figured since it was only going to be Mindi and her mother there, you wouldn't have an objection. It seemed to be Mr. Braemarie that worried you. So ... the excitement of spending time with a new friend and seeing horses won out over obeying you.

Sorry.

"I'd love to!" I answered, brightly.

Mom easily bought my story about going for a long bike ride because I was in training for basketball, but I felt a sharp twinge of guilt at lying to her — honestly.

Mindi waved to me from her seat on the shady front porch of the old brick house. I dropped my bike, bounded up the steps, and plopped down in one of the empty chairs. A plate of cookies and a pitcher of lemonade sat on a small table between us. Very country-ish, I thought.

"Hey, that was fast," greeted Mindi. She gestured to the cookies. I helped myself enthusiastically. From inside the house, I could hear a woman humming.

"That's my mom," Mindi explained. "She always hums when she's in a good mood. She's been here all day, painting, so I'm surprised she stopped long enough to bake these cookies. She's been working pretty hard lately trying to get ready for her next exhibit."

"That's neat, having a mom who's an artist," I commented around a mouthful of cookie.

Mindi shrugged. "I guess, but she gets so focused sometimes, like now, that I hardly get a chance to talk to her. But I suppose it's better than before. After she and my dad split up she didn't paint at all. She said her 'muse' had vanished. Then she met Colin and she started to paint again — when she's here. She says the farm setting is idyllic and inspires her. So that's why I get to bus here so many days after school. It's actually a pretty cool set-up."

We finished off the cookies and lemonade, then Mindi led me around the back of the house toward the stable, chatting about the horses the whole time. She seemed genuinely excited to have me there. The stable doors seemed wider and the manure smells stronger from this side of the raspberry bushes. As we entered, a soft whinny greeted us, and I soon forgot about the offending odours in anticipation of meeting real, live horses.

Inside the stable was more spacious than I expected. The horse stalls were along the wall facing us as we entered. Bare light bulbs jutted out high on the walls between them. Two horses were peeking out over their stall doors, eyeing us. A small room — I later learned it was called the tack room — was to the right of the stable doors. An old freezer and bundles of hay were stored along the wall on the other side of the tack room. To the left of us, bags of wood shavings were stacked, flanked by pitchforks, rakes, and the old wheelbarrow that I'd watched Mr. Braemarie using.

Mindi hurried over to the nearest horse and crooned, "Look at you poor things, stuck inside all day." To me, she explained, "Usually Colin turns them out into the fenced field on nice days, but he hasn't been home today so he kept them in."

As Mindi put halters on the horses so she could lead them outside, she introduced me to them. First, there was Ginger. She was a gentle chestnut-coloured horse with a white diamond on her forehead. At Mindi's urging, I nervously reached out to stroke between Ginger's eyes. To my amazement, Ginger nuzzled into my hand.

"She's so friendly!" I exclaimed.

Mindi nodded. "I knew you'd like her. This is my mom's favourite. She's so gentle and easygoing. She'll be the perfect horse for you to learn on — if you want to."

"Sure!" I was beaming. This was so cool! I was actually going to ride a horse. Eagerly, I followed Mindi to the next stall, where I was introduced to Candy, another mare.

"Candy's my favourite," Mindi whispered, as though trying not to hurt the other horses' feelings. Candy's dark brown coat gleamed and she stamped her finely muscled front legs. She wasn't quite as friendly with me as Ginger. She tossed her head teasingly each time I reached out to pet her.

"Try buttering her up with an apple or a carrot stick," laughed Mindi, pulling a chunk of carrot out of her jacket pocket. "Hold your hand flat, so she won't nibble your fingers." I did as I was told, and to my delight, Candy leaned down and snuffled up the chunk of carrot on my hand. I laughed and stroked her between the eyes as she crunched.

The next stall was Thunder's. He was noisily slurping water from a bucket. His long, black tail swished back and forth at our approach, as if in irritation.

"Thunder," called Mindi, "come and meet a friend of mine."

Snorting, Thunder pulled his head out of the water bucket. Water slopped from his mouth as he eyed us. His black coat gleamed, and his black mane was so perfect it looked recently combed.

"I have to be a bit more careful around Thunder," said Mindi. "He tries to nip at my arms and legs when

I groom him. Colin says that's his way of testing me, and I'm not supposed to let him."

"Oh," I said, backing away from the stall door. I didn't like the sound of a biting horse.

Mindi laughed. "He's not that bad. He's just full of spirit. Colin says he likes riding him because he's a challenge."

"Did I just hear my name?" said a deep voice from behind us.

Mindi and I jumped. Mindi's eyes doubled in sized and her mouth gaped open. My own heart leaped in my chest; I wasn't supposed to be there. We were busted. The manure-shovelling man stood in the wide doorway of the stable, hands on his hips.

"Hi, Colin. You're home early," stammered Mindi, shifting from one foot to the other.

"Yes, I am. Surprise, surprise, eh? I see you have a friend over." He wasn't smiling.

"Uh, Colin, this is Sarah Martin, the girl I told you about. Her family just moved into the Browns' old house. Sarah, this is Colin Braemarie."

"Nice to meet you, Mr. Braemarie," I said. "I love your horses." That was my lame attempt to be charming.

"Sarah's going to help with the horses, Colin," said Mindi. "It's great having someone here with me, so I don't have to do this all alone."

"Yes, I guess it is," he said.

Mindi and Mr. Braemarie exchanged a look, you know, one of those looks that's loaded with meaning. I figured that his said, *I told you not to bring anyone over here!* While hers said, *What's the big deal? We're not going to get in your way.* Apparently, Mindi won him over because Mr. Braemarie turned to me and gave me a grimace which I think was meant to be a smile.

"I see you've met Thunder," he said, stepping up to the stall door and scratching the black horse behind the ears. "He's a good old boy, aren't you, Thunder?"

"I was going to tack up Ginger and Candy after we clean out the stalls," said Mindi. "Is that okay, Colin?" She gave him a hopeful smile.

He sighed. "Just make sure you wear helmets. I have extra ones in the tack room that Sarah can use."

Mindi brightened and mouthed, "Yes!" to me as she followed him into the tack room.

Mr. Braemarie pulled out a dusty trunk from the back of the room. It was full of helmets and tall boots. "These were all left here when I moved in," he explained. He fished around and pulled out a dusty black helmet. "This should do the trick. Try this on, Sarah, it's not pretty but it'll keep your head safe."

It fit. I gushed my thanks to Mr. Braemarie.

"So, you'll just stay in the fenced field?" he asked Mindi, his forehead creased with worry.

"Yes, we will," she answered, nodding vigorously. "I'm going to teach Sarah some basics."

"You won't go near the barn?"

"No, we'll just stay in the fenced field. Sarah's never ridden before."

"Okay. You're okay with all this, Sarah? Mindi's trying to turn you into a horse-crazy girl, like her?" I nodded vigorously and watched the lines on his forehead disappear. "Remember your helmets, then, and keep

Sarah on Ginger — she's the best to learn on," he said gruffly. "Call me if you need any help."

"Don't worry, Colin. We'll be fine," assured Mindi.

"C'mon, Sarah," she called over her shoulder as she led Candy out of the stable towards the field. "Grab a pitchfork. Let's get these stalls mucked out so we can ride."

"Okay," I said. I gingerly lifted a pitchfork off its peg on the wall and wondered what I was supposed to do with it.

"Sarah," Mr. Braemarie said quietly once Mindi was out of earshot. The creases on his forehead were back. "I have some rules here," he began. "In addition to wearing helmets while riding, the old barn out back is strictly off limits." He cleared his throat. "I have some heavy, expensive equipment out there that can be dangerous so I don't let anyone near it — okay?"

I nodded. "Okay. No problem."

He stared at me for a moment, the forehead crease deepening. "You're sure you're not going to have a problem with that rule? I can't let Mindi have friends over who might mess around in there. It's just too dangerous."

"I promise I won't go near it," I assured him. He was freaking me out a little by then. Why was he so hyper about that stupid barn?

He gave me a curt nod that I took as a dismissal. I hurried into Candy's empty stall with my pitchfork and started plunging it into the shavings, eager to show him my willingness to help out. I wanted a return visit.

I felt Mr. Braemarie's eyes watching me. He sighed and took the pitchfork from me. "Like this, Sarah."

I watched as he showed me how to pick the waste out of the shavings and dump it into a wheelbarrow. Then he gave me back the pitchfork and watched as I took over. I put my back into my work and tried my best to impress him. By the time I finished the stall, he was gone. I hadn't noticed him leaving.

"Are you going to be in trouble because of me?" I asked Mindi as I pushed my full wheelbarrow past Ginger and Thunder's clean stalls on my way to the manure pile.

Mindi shrugged. "Nah. He'll be okay — he's a good guy, his bark's worse than his bite."

"While you were taking Candy out to the field, he told me that we had to stay away from the barn."

Mindi groaned. "That stupid barn. Ever since he bought all that antique farm machinery he's been frantic about my mom or me going near it and getting hurt. Why he'd even think I'd be interested is beyond me. It's not like I'm some dorky little kid who'd want to climb all over machines and stuff."

"Has he ever shown you the antiques?" I asked.

"No, he hasn't," she frowned. "Maybe I should ask for a tour. You'd think he'd want to show them off. He spends enough time out there 'cause he loves them so much." She waved her hand in the air. "Oh well, who cares? It's just old junk, anyway."

She grabbed two lead lines off their pegs and handed one to me. "Let's get Candy and Ginger back here. I'll show you how to tack up a horse — to put on its saddle and bridle so you can ride it."

While we were walking out to the field, Mindi said, "You know, I never really thought about it much before now, but he's *always* telling me to stay away from that barn. *All the time.* Making me promise and everything. It's like he's obsessed or something.

"And lately he's had a lot of antique dealers coming out here at night," Mindi added as we led our horses back into the stable. "So he makes us go home. It's kinda weird."

"Huh, that is kind of weird," I agreed with a nod.

Mindi shrugged. "I mean, who cares if you have to do a little business? My mom and I would stay out of his way. But my mom just goes along with it, she always makes sure we're out of the way by the time any dealers arrive. She says that Colin would be too uptight if we were around and that he wants to keep his personal life out of his business."

Let me tell you, my investigator's senses were tingling like crazy. I wondered if I should tell Mindi about the Braemarie file I found in Dad's briefcase. Would antique farm machinery warrant a police file? Were they stolen goods? I decided to bite my tongue. After all, what did I really know? Nothing. For all I knew it could have nothing to do with her mom's boyfriend. There are other Braemaries in the world. No sense getting Mindi worried about nothing.

Before too long, I was standing on a stool putting one foot into a stirrup and swinging a leg over the back of Ginger as per Mindi's directions. Then I was sitting. Me, on a horse! It was weird, but cool — very cool.

I had such a good time walking around in the fenced field on Ginger that my curiosity about Mr. Braemarie and his mysterious barn was momentarily forgotten.

Momentarily.

I shared that last section of the report with Mindi on the bus today. She wasn't too happy to find out that I knew about your police file on Mr. Braemarie and didn't tell her about it. I explained to her that I didn't want to alarm her over nothing. After all, I had no idea what was in that file, thanks to Roy (don't get me started!). It could have been anything from tax fraud to a land dispute. I wasn't going to assume the worst, say for instance that Mr. Braemarie was into stolen goods. Even though this was my main theory at the time.

The thing that was most obvious was that I needed to get a look at whatever was in that barn!

You sure acted like you were suspicious of me when I got back from the farmhouse that day. I felt like one of your perps. Once you stopped freaking out about me getting home late from my "bike ride," I was able to give you my story about how I crashed my bike trying to ride on these stupid pot-holed country roads. I think you fell for it — even though I'm really sorry I had to give you a cover story. (You should have just let me go over there legally!)

Unfortunately, Roy didn't fall for my story as easily as you, Dad. He cornered me later and made me tell him the truth. I ended up getting blabby — maybe Roy should give you tips on interrogation — and I even told him about what Mr. Braemarie said to me about the barn. Of course, he threatened to go right to you and rat me out but I stopped him by promising to make his bed every day for the next week.

Isn't that extortion, Dad?

By the way, I'm sure you'll be happy to know that the day after my illegal horseback-riding lesson, I was very sore. My back ached, my thighs ached, even my fingers hurt. Worst of all, I had fallen off Ginger and landed in a pile of manure. The bruise on my butt made it very uncomfortable to sit in classes all day. You couldn't have punished me better yourself.

The rest of the week was uneventful, but the following Monday, Mindi invited me back to the farmhouse to go horseback riding again. Sorry to say, Dad, but my life was so boring, and my first visit was so much fun, I couldn't resist going. Besides, I was so desperate to have a friend wanting to spend time with me that there was really no way I could say no. I realize you won't think that's a good enough reason for disobeying you — but, at the time, I did.

Try not to get mad all over again when you read this, Dad. You wanted to know it all, remember? This report wasn't my idea. Maybe the old saying "Ignorance is bliss" is true?

Back Again

Date: Monday, September 17

Location: The Forbidden Barn

As soon as the school bus dropped me off, I threw my knapsack in the door, yelled to my mom that I was going for a bike ride, and took off without even giving her a chance to object. I was riding my bike out of the garage when Roy blocked my way.

"Where do you think you're going in such a hurry?" he asked.

"What do you care?" I retorted.

I tried to wheel around him, but he grabbed firmly onto my handlebars.

"I don't think you should be going to that farmhouse," he said, then held up his hand at my protest. "I know that's where you're going. Mom and Dad may be dumb enough to buy your two-hour bike ride stories, but I'm not."

Honestly, Dad, that's what he said. His exact words.

"Just listen to me for once," he continued. "Dad

wouldn't tell you not to go over there without a good reason. You should listen to him; it might not be safe."

I gave him my best stage smile. "Roy! I never knew you cared. How touching."

"Cut it out, Sarah! I'm serious. You shouldn't be going over there."

"C'mon, Roy. What exactly do you think could happen? Mindi's there all the time, and she's just fine. The boogeyman hasn't got her. Besides, all we're going to do is hang out in the stable and then ride the horses for a bit. There's nothing to worry about. I'll be back before dinner," I said, sounding, for once, like the voice of reason.

"What about that old barn you told me about?" he persisted, still holding onto my handlebars. "The one Mr. Braemarie warned you to stay away from."

"We don't go anywhere near that." I waved him off. "Besides it's just full of antique farm equipment and machinery. There's nothing to worry about."

He frowned, then finally stepped aside to let me pass. "I should probably tell Dad about this."

"I'll keep making your bed for you," I crooned, batting my eyelashes at him.

He grinned. He couldn't help it, I was so charming.

"Just be careful over there," he said. "And ..."

I sighed. Would his nagging ever end?

"... if anything weird happens, and I mean anything, come straight home."

"Oh, Roy, relax. Nothing's going to happen," I said, as I pushed past him and wheeled down the driveway. "And the only weird thing around here is you!"

"I mean it, Sarah. Come home if anything is weird!" he yelled.

"Eat my dust, Roy!" I yelled back. Jeeesh! And people say I'm nosy.

Mindi was pacing on the porch when I biked down the long driveway to the farmhouse. She ran down the stairs to greet me. I barely set my feet on the ground when she grabbed my arm.

"Quick, Sarah," she urged. "Let's go straight to the stable. I have to talk to you."

Caught up in her excitement, I dropped my bike and ran with her to the stable. Once there, Mindi shut the large doors behind us. I turned to her eagerly.

"I'm so glad you're here, Sarah. I really need to talk to someone about this," she said, grabbing my arm once again.

"What's going on?" I asked.

"I think Colin's into something weird," she burst out. "Illegal, I mean."

"Really?" I asked, swallowing hard at her use of the word *weird*. Roy's parting words started to echo in my head. "What makes you think that?"

Mindi's eyes darted nervously around the stable as if worried about the horses overhearing.

"I got off the bus and came into the house, as usual. Mom was painting in the back room, so I didn't bug her. I headed to the den to let Colin know I was here. He was on the phone, so I was about to go out to the stable when I overheard what he was saying. It seemed kind of weird, so I stayed at the door and listened."

"What was he saying?" I asked, wincing when she said the word *weird* again. Roy was having a fit in my head.

"He said something about his products being one hundred percent genuine articles and how you wouldn't find better quality anywhere else in Ontario. He said that he didn't want to talk anymore on his home phone, and that if they wanted to do business with him, they had to come see him in person. He set up a time to meet them at five o'clock today. Then he turned around and saw me in the hallway. You should have seen the look on his face. He was so mad! He slammed the door right in my face."

"Whoa."

"Don't you think that's weird?"

"Very," I nodded, wishing she would stop saying that word.

"He's never gotten angry with me like that before. He actually *slammed* the door right in my face. Why would he do that? Why would some old farm equipment in an old barn make him so crazy? Is that what's really in there?" She chewed her thumbnail, looking at me, waiting for answers, I guess. I didn't have any. As far as I was concerned, this confirmed what I already suspected. There was something fishy about Mr. Braemarie and that barn!

"I want to know what's really in that barn," Mindi announced, as if reading my thoughts. "I want to know what he meant by one hundred percent genuine articles. Whoever Colin was talking to on the phone is coming here at five o'clock and I'm going to be out at that barn to hear what they have to say."

So that's how it came about. You see? I didn't go over to the farmhouse looking for trouble, but, as usual, trouble found me. I really had no choice; I had to help my new friend. I couldn't abandon her during her moment of need. If I didn't go to the barn with her, she'd have gone by herself, and what kind of person would abandon a friend like that? Right?

Once Mindi knew we were in this together, she ordered us to work. We broke into a frenzy of activity. The stalls had to be quickly mucked out before we could tack up the horses for our spy mission. Mindi had a plan. By the time I finished Ginger's stall, Mindi had cleaned both Thunder's and Candy's stalls and was leading Candy in from the field.

I was just bringing Ginger in from the field, and Mindi was putting a saddle on Candy, when Mr. Braemarie stepped into the stable. His huge frame filled the doorway. He didn't look happy.

"You're supposed to clean stalls before tacking up horses," he said, gruffly.

"We're done cleaning stalls," Mindi clipped, without interrupting her flow of adjusting and buckling the saddle strap. "I'm giving Sarah another lesson. If she does as well as last time, we're going to do a trail ride."

Mr. Braemarie cleared his throat and shuffled from foot to foot, watching Mindi work. Finally he said in a gentler tone of voice, "Can I talk to you outside for a minute?"

Mindi shrugged and stepped outside behind him. I thought again of Roy's warning that if anything weird happened, I should come straight home, and I actually considered doing just that as I stood waiting. Then, tired of just dumbly standing there, I grabbed Ginger's bridle off the peg in the tack room and tried my darndest to put the bit into her mouth the way Mindi had showed me. I was covered in horse slobber and still struggling when Mindi and Mr. Braemarie came back. Mindi had a triumphant grin on her face, while Mr. Braemarie looked like he'd just been pinched — hard.

"Don't *worry*, Colin," Mindi was saying, "Sarah and I will either be here or on the trail. We won't interfere with your visitors."

"Humph," he grunted, while he wordlessly took the bridle from me and easily slipped the bit into Ginger's mouth.

Out in the fenced field, Mindi, true to her word, gave me my second lesson. I learned how to position my feet properly in the stirrups, with my heels down, and how to do a rising trot. There's a lot more to riding than meets the eye. I had no idea. I thought you just climbed up and held on. Then, with a glance at her watch, Mindi announced that I was ready to hit the trail.

"Ginger knows it really well. She'll just follow Candy so all you really have to do is sit there," Mindi explained.

This made me feel better, because I have to admit, I was more than a little nervous about leaving the fenced field. I had visions of my horse bolting, galloping to who knew where, with me holding on for dear life — or worse, flying off and landing in a broken heap.

Of course, I wasn't about to tell Mindi that. She didn't seem to be afraid of anything when it came to horses.

We walked along the trail in silence for a while. Mindi was right, Ginger did just follow Candy. I started to relax and enjoy the ride. I was actually getting used to sitting on a horse and so was rather impressed with myself. I'd never get a chance to do this if I still lived in Mississauga. Maybe country living wasn't so bad after all. Except there aren't any decent malls, of course.

"Colin wanted Mom and me to go home," Mindi said, breaking the silence. "We went back to the house, that's what took us so long. But I talked him into letting us stay, since I already had Candy all ready and the stalls all cleaned." She chuckled without humour. "I think Colin was afraid I was going to say something to my mom about how he slammed the door in my face. You should have heard him apologizing when we were walking back to the house ..." she shook her head. "Whatever. Anyway, it took a bit of convincing but I finally got him to let us stay and ride — provided we don't leave this trail or the stable while his 'guests' are here. It helped that Mom was right into a creative idea and it's hard to stop her from painting when she's like that."

She turned to me, and her brown eyes glinted in the late afternoon sun that streamed through the trees.

"We're not going to stay on this trail, are we?" I asked.

"Nope."

"Are you sure about this?"

"Yes." Her face was set. "I have to know what he's up to with these so-called guests in that stupid barn.

What's making him so uptight? He slammed a door in my face!" She stared at me, daring me to argue with her. I didn't.

I'd like to be able to tell you, Dad, that I tried harder to talk Mindi out of this little spy expedition, really I would. But that wouldn't be honest. The truth is, I was every bit as curious as she was about the mysterious barn and Mr. Braemarie's guests. I was thrilled to be in the middle of this adventure with her.

Apparently, the trail was one big loop through the bush, so once we were in there far enough to be well hidden, we slid off the horses, tied them to a couple of trees with the lead lines Mindi had brought, and cut through the woods to come up alongside the old barn. We hunkered down behind a couple of thick old trees and peeked out. Even this close, the barn looked completely harmless. The best word to describe its appearance was dilapidated (I had to use that word in a sentence in English class the other day). It was basically a large box with a rough gray barn board exterior that had seen much better days. The roof was a dull brownish red. Small dirty windows were placed high, near the roof. The door was kept shut by a large metal padlock.

Mindi glanced at her watch. "It's 4:56," she whispered. "They should be here any minute."

Right on cue, Mr. Braemarie came marching briskly along the long, dirt driveway leading up to the barn, motioning a black car forward. It looked like the same one that I'd seen there a couple of weeks before. I just about leaned towards Mindi to tell her so but stopped myself in time. She had no idea that I had already sat in almost this exact spot and spied on the goings-on at this barn. The car pulled ahead and parked. Mr. Braemarie jogged up to it, casting glances all around. I prayed the trees were hiding us well enough.

Three men stepped out of the car. Again, they were dressed in dark suits; I vaguely wondered if there was a dress code at the old forbidden barn. I recognized two of them. The drill sergeant and the laughing man. The third man, who I hadn't seen before, was tall and lanky. His face had a pebbly look and he moved around restlessly as he stood. Mr. Braemarie spoke to the laughing man.

"Welcome, once again, Mr. Gorely," he said, shaking his hand. Gorely's heavy rings caught the light of the lowering sun and flashed as their hands shook.

"Mr. Braemarie," nodded Gorely. "You remember Mr. Cheng ..." he indicated the drill sergeant with a wave of his hand, "... and this is Mr. Morchan." Hands were shaken all around.

"So, you've been here a few times now," said Mr. Braemarie to Gorely. "I take it that you're definitely interested in my little operation."

"I've spoken with my people and, yes, we are very interested in your proposal for business. There are many restaurants and pharmaceutical companies that are willing to pay excellent money for what you have. In fact, we have one influential client in particular who is most interested in buying your products. But first, my colleague ..." he nodded towards the fidgety, pebbly-faced man "... wanted to have a look at the product himself so that we can assure our customer, with full confidence, that the quality is exceptional."

Gorely's voice had a steel edge to it that made me shiver, in spite of his smiling face.

"Of course," said Mr. Braemarie. "I'm sure you'll be satisfied, Mr. Morchan. I'll give you a tour, then we'll discuss the terms of purchase." Morchan nodded briskly, while his eyes darted around restlessly at the three men.

Mr. Braemarie pulled a key out of his pocket and unlocked the padlock securing the barn door. He pushed it open, hung the padlock on the unbolted metal loop, then, addressing all three men, he said, "If you gentlemen would please follow me." They all stepped inside and the door swung shut behind them.

I was speechless. Mesmerized. Those men definitely didn't seem to be the type to be interested in antique farming equipment. I wondered what they were really there for. We waited in silence behind those trees for what seemed forever. Mindi's face was pale, her eyes wide. I wondered what she was thinking. There was nothing to say, nothing to see, yet there was no way we could leave while those men were in that barn. Finally, after what seemed like an eternity, the door opened. Morchan, the pebbly-faced man, was talking as they filed out.

"You have quite the set-up in there, Mr. Braemarie," he said, his hand beating a rhythm against his leg. His voice was unexpectedly deep, coming out of such a twiggy body.

"I think we'll be able to work out a very satisfactory deal," said Gorely.

"Most definitely," nodded Mr. Braemarie, with a tight smile. "Now, as I was saying, my prices for parts are non-negotiable. I know I might be a bit higher than other suppliers, but my parts are guaranteed to be genuine. Besides, this business is riskier than it used to be, and I need to take care of my profit margin."

"I understand," said Gorely, nodding. "I'll talk to my buyers and be back with our initial order by the end of the week."

"Sounds good. I look forward to your next visit. You know how to reach me," said Mr. Braemarie as they shook hands. Gorely slipped into the passenger seat of the car, his rings catching the last low rays of the sun.

Morchan shook Mr. Braemarie's hand also, a vigorous two pumps as if he were either trying to impress Mr. Braemarie or hurt him. Mr. Braemarie didn't appear to notice.

"We'll be in touch," said Morchan, with that surprisingly deep voice. The drill sergeant, Cheng, simply got in behind the wheel of the black car. Apparently, he didn't do much talking.

Mr. Braemarie stood and watched as the car backed down the driveway and drove out of sight. He started to walk back into the barn but stopped himself, then turned and looked all around before briskly jogging to the house, leaving the barn door unlocked — beckoning and inviting me. It was an opportunity that was too good to be true!

Startled, Mindi and I looked at each other.

"He left the barn door open," I pointed out, needlessly. "I thought he always kept it locked."

"He does ..."

"Here's our chance. We can go inside and see what's in there."

Mindi hesitated. "I don't know, Sarah … What do you think they meant by 'genuine parts'?"

"There's only one way to find out." I tugged at her arm and started towards the barn.

She pulled back. "I can't. I'm scared."

"There's nothing to be scared of. Those men are gone. Come on," I urged. She still hung back. Some people are just not cut out for detective work. "We'll never get a chance like this again! We have to go for it," I pleaded.

I had already wasted valuable time. With a quick look towards the house to make sure the coast was still clear, I made the dash to the barn as fast as my feet could carry me. I vaguely remember Mindi grabbing my arm. Nobody could stop me, I was on a mission. This was a golden opportunity. If Mindi didn't want to join me, that was her choice.

No sooner had I slipped into the barn than I heard the distant slamming of the house door. Mr. Braemarie was coming back! So soon! Now *I* was scared. I pressed my hands to my chest to calm my hammering heart; I had to think fast. At any moment, he would be walking through that door, and the last thing I wanted him to see was me standing there holding onto my heart.

My frantic eyes darted around the small room and ended up on a rickety old ladder leaning against the wall on my left. It led up to a loft. I went for it and climbed the rungs with lightning speed. Just as I reached the top, Mr. Braemarie walked in. I scrambled behind the sweet-smelling bundled hay that filled almost the entire loft and worked on slowing my breathing.

At first I was too frightened to move. I couldn't believe what I had done! What was I thinking? Roy always accuses me of being impulsive — maybe he has a point. I longed to be outside again with Mindi, innocently hiding behind trees, safely heading back to the horses.

It was gloomy up in the loft. There was one tiny, filthy window that allowed some murky outside light to seep in. The only other source of light was from the room below, where Mr. Braemarie sat. Beyond the sweet smell of the hay, there was a rank smell, like you'd find at a zoo, filling the air, making me wrinkle my nose.

Slowly, I inched forward until I could peek around the stacks of hay. The first thing I saw was the top of Mr. Braemarie's head. He had a small bald spot that I hadn't noticed before. The light from the bare overhead bulb glinted off it and made it stand out against his cropped blond hair. He sat at a large, neatly organized desk covered with the usual desk stuff, you know, a phone, file folders, clock, pens, and so on. He was reading the contents of a thick file. There were two other chairs in the room, facing the desk. Otherwise, the small room was empty.

Eventually, Mr. Braemarie stopped flipping through the file in front of him and reached into his open jacket. With a slight twist he pulled something out and set it on the desk in front of him with a thump. It was a gun. I sucked in my breath. The only people I know who have guns are cops — and they're allowed. Mr. Braemarie fiddled with the weapon, dumping something into his hand — I assumed it was the bullets. He swiftly tucked the gun into the bottom drawer of the desk.

I swallowed hard, and the sound seemed to fill the entire hayloft. I froze, afraid to move. My head spun. What on Earth was I doing here? What would Mr. Braemarie do to me if he found me hiding here? He obviously wasn't the nice guy that Mindi and her mom thought he was. What kind of nice guy keeps a gun in his desk? For that matter, who keeps a desk in an old barn? What kind of operation was he running here? Why hadn't I listened to Dad and Roy and stayed away?

Mr. Braemarie snatched up a cell phone and punched in some numbers. After a pause, he barked into the mouthpiece. "It's Colin. Gorely and his thugs were here and everything went as planned." He paused. "End of the week." Another pause. "Gotcha. No problem."

He tucked the phone into his shirt pocket. Sighing deeply, he stood up and stretched. Then he left the barn, slamming the door. The decisive click of the padlock that I heard all the way up in the gloomy hayloft made my blood run cold.

I was locked inside the *forbidden* barn.

I'll tell you, Dad, I never planned to go into the forbidden barn, never mind getting myself locked inside. Mindi and I only wanted to take a look at Mr. Braemarie's visitors to get an idea about what he was selling. Simple as that. Why do I always have to be so impulsive?

So that's the situation I found myself in. Locked in a barn. Me, a city girl! There was nothing I could do at that point but investigate!

Trapped!

Date: Monday, September 17 (continued)

Location: Still in the Forbidden Barn

I felt like screaming — in fact I think my mouth opened to do so — but then the rattling door and Mindi's voice stopped me.

"Sarah?"

I stumbled down from the hayloft. "Mindi! I can't get out!" I said, trying in vain to keep my voice level. "I'm locked in."

"I know," Mindi groaned.

"Mindi! What are we going to do?" I pleaded.

"I don't know." Mindi moaned again. "Is there any other way out?"

I swallowed down a sob and looked around the room. "There's a door," I said. "It leads to the back of the barn. Maybe there's a way out back there."

"Okay," said Mindi, "I'll check around the outside. I've never been this close to the barn before. Maybe there's another door around the back." She sounded skeptical.

I walked over to the only other door in the small room. Whatever lay beyond was what brought those men out here. This was why I sneaked into the barn. I should have been excited, but instead I only wanted to find a way out. Slowly, I pushed open the heavy door.

The room was dim. The only light seemed to come from the ceiling skylights, and I blinked, trying to make out the large, vague shapes inside. The air was humid, and the zoo-like animal smell I'd noticed earlier was much stronger. I stepped through the door.

The room was huge, taking up the rest of the barn. My eyes were slow to adjust to the light but I could see that large cages lined both walls to my right and left. They seemed to cover the entire length of the barn, forming a wide corridor between them. I approached the first one to my right. The door was ajar, and I peeked inside. An upturned wheelbarrow was wedged into the corner, a coiled-up garden hose hanging on a hook beside it. I stepped inside the cage to get a better look. I lifted the wooden lid of one of the two half barrels beside the hose. I wrinkled my nose in disgust at the pig slop inside. The bag of ice thrown on top did nothing to stop the stench. I knew all about pig slop since my mom kept telling us how much pigs loved the slop left over on our plates after dinner. An ancient-looking fridge hummed beside the barrels. I pulled open the heavy door latch. It was full of open plastic tubs holding huge chunks of stinky raw chicken and fish. Ugh! I held my nose and pushed the door closed, hearing the latch click loudly. Who — or what — was eating all this nasty food?

I suddenly became aware of soft snuffling sounds. A hulking dark form moved in the cage beside me. My stomach turned to ice. I took a step towards it. When I was close enough to touch the bars, the dark form grunted and moved, surprisingly quickly. A large hairy face swung my way. I stifled a scream and jumped back. A black, glistening nose shoved its way between the cage bars and busily sniffed the air. I took another startled step back before realizing that I was looking at a bear. A huge black bear standing on its back legs and sniffing furiously at me.

I backed out of the cage and stood in the corridor, rooted. It was as if the world had suddenly stopped turning on its axis. My eyes, completely accustomed now to the dark room, examined the rows of cages with fascination. They were large and spacious, similar to what you'd see at a zoo. I counted six cages along either side of the barn walls. Assuming one bear per cage, minus the cage with the food, that made eleven bears. Wow.

The bear on my left became quite agitated by my presence. It swung its massive head to and fro, peering down its long nose at me. The bear to my right still had its snout pushed through the cage bars. I was frozen, amazed.

A loud knocking from the end of the barn pulled me out of my reverie. I jumped.

"Sarah!" It was Mindi's muffled voice from outside. "Can you hear me?"

"Just barely," I yelled. The bears, startled by my voice, grunted and shuffled in their cages.

"Did you find a way out?" she asked.

"No, not yet. You wouldn't believe what's in here, Mindi," I yelled. "You have to see this."

"Never mind that now, Sarah, it's getting late. We've got to get you out of there. Colin's going to wonder why we're not back with the horses soon."

"Oh, right," I mumbled. How could I have forgotten about that? I looked up at the skylights in the barn's ceiling. The sky wasn't as bright as I hoped it still was. Suddenly, the barn seemed spooky in the growing gloom. What if I couldn't get out and I had to spend the night? The thought of being trapped in there alone, in the dark, with a bunch of wild bears made my knees start to tremble. The fact that they were in cages didn't seem to make me feel a whole lot better.

"I can't find any other doors, Sarah," Mindi said, her voice fading as she talked, as if she were walking away from me.

I was cooked. There was no way out. I was beginning to resign myself to the fact that I'd be bunking down with the bears when I heard banging; Mindi was up to something.

"I found a spot where there are some rotting boards; I may be able to break them and make an opening for you to crawl through!" yelled Mindi in a muffled voice, now from the far end of the barn and to my left. The sharp crack of splintering wood made the bears shift restlessly within their cages.

"Can you give me a hand from the inside?" asked Mindi, sounding a bit winded. "These boards are tougher than they look."

"I'll try," I called. The two bears on either side of me grunted as if skeptical I could be of any help to anyone. They were probably right.

I stared down the middle corridor of the long barn. I didn't particularly relish the idea of walking in the dark between cages of wild bears, but I had no choice if I wanted to get to Mindi.

With a quick prayer for strong bars, I put one foot forward. The barn now had more shadows than light, and the bears seemed to grow more and more restless with any movement. I put the other foot ahead of the first. The end of the corridor seemed to move farther away. Honestly, it did! I swallowed. The bears were like hulking monsters in the shadows. I felt their eyes following my every move.

"Don't be stupid, Sarah ... don't be stupid, Sarah ..." I chanted softly. Sometimes I let my imagination run away with me — this was one of those times. I swallowed again and forced another foot to go forward, all the while acutely aware of every sound: the bears rustling and snorting, the soft thump of my tentative steps, the heavy pounding of my heart, and my ragged breathing. I focused on walking exactly in the middle of the corridor so that I was as far away as possible from the cages on either side.

I had taken about half a dozen steps when a bear to my right grunted. Another grunted, as if in answer. These two bears were joined by several others until soon there was a cacophony of madly grunting bears marking my painfully slow voyage down the corridor. I put my hands over my ears and stumbled on. Suddenly, a bear to my left reared onto its hind legs and slid its long, thick claws through the cage bars, reaching for me. I yelled and jumped back, hitting the bars of the cage behind me hard. An impossibly loud roar exploded in my ear. I whirled to face a massive open mouth crammed with gleaming yellow teeth. I froze in horror as the roar filled the barn and deafened me.

Finally, the mouth snapped shut and its owner charged towards me, hurtling himself against the flimsy bars of his cage. I screamed and fled towards the far end of the barn. With a thud, I hit the wall and collapsed in a heap on the floor, my arms up to shield myself from the inevitable mauling I was about to receive.

"Sarah! What's going on in there?" Mindi shrieked from outside the barn. "It sounds like a pack of wild animals are on the loose!"

I lowered my arms and laughed deliriously. Oh yeah, Mindi. There were wild animals in here all right, and to my immense relief, the cage bars were stronger than they looked because no bears had busted loose to chase me down.

"Sarah? Are you all right?"

"I'm okay," I replied, weakly. "I'll live." That made me giggle. I think I was getting a bit hysterical. I do that sometimes.

The bears were quieting down now that I was sitting still on the floor. The closer ones watched me sullenly as if daring me to make a move. I stayed there for a while, on alert for a possible attack, oblivious to the cold seeping into my bottom. I slowly became aware of the sounds of Mindi breaking off rotting bits of the outside barn board in her efforts to free me. One part of me understood that I was being stupid. After all, the bears were in cages, they couldn't hurt me. But another part of me was totally freaked out. I finally stood up, slowly sliding my back up the rough wall as I rose.

"Sarah! Where are you? I could use your help here," Mindi gasped.

"I think I'm the one who needs the help, Mindi," I said. That almost set off another round of hysterical giggling, but I managed to stop myself.

"What did you say, Sarah?" asked Mindi.

"I'll be right there," I answered, not wanting to explain myself at that moment.

A few bears snorted more protests at the sounds of our voices, but other than that they seemed to have calmed down. I guess they were getting used to me.

"I'm still working on this rotten board," Mindi said, her voice strained. "I'm trying to break off enough of it so that you can squeeze through the hole. So far, I've only broken off small chunks, but I think I can do better."

I could hear the sound of splintering wood nearby as Mindi spoke, and I almost cried with relief. I knew I couldn't survive a whole night alone in that barn with the bears. I wasn't even up to another walk between their cages.

"Can you find me, Sarah? Follow my voice, I'm over here."

Mindi's voice was coming from outside the far wall of the barn, behind the cages, to my right. Keeping my back to the wall, I slowly made my way along it towards the corner of the barn. As I went, I listened to Mindi's grunts of exertion as she worked on breaking the rotting barn boards loose. When I reached the pitch black corner of the barn, I had to face the realization that in order to get any closer to Mindi and freedom I'd have to squeeze into the small space between the cages and the outer barn wall.

"Mindi?" I called.

"I'm here, keep coming. You sound closer."

"Are you sure there isn't a different rotting board somewhere else on this old barn?" I asked.

"Are you nuts? I've been all around this place at least four or five times. I'm lucky I found this one. Besides, it's starting to get dark, we've got to hurry." She paused. "Why? What's wrong?" Her voice was flat.

My heart sank. "Nothing. Never mind, I'm coming."

I gulped and then entered the narrow passage between the last cage and the outer barn wall. I flattened myself against the wall as much as possible and began to slowly shuffle myself along.

"Think thin," I told myself over and over again.

"Are you saying something, Sarah?" asked Mindi, her voice sounding closer and clearer than ever.

"No, nothing."

As I continued to edge myself along, I felt the hot breath of a bear sniffing at my legs through the bars of its cage. We were becoming real good friends, the bears and me. I smothered another hysterical giggle. I couldn't believe that I was that close to a real bear. At that point, I was actually thankful for the darkness. That way, I couldn't see all the sets of eyes that were undoubtedly watching my slow journey to freedom.

"Those bars should be closer together," I muttered as a nose pressed through to sniff at me. I was their entertainment for the evening, I guess. Better than satellite TV.

"What did you say? Did you say bars?" asked Mindi. Her voice came from just a short distance ahead.

"Just get me out of here, I'll explain later," I urged.

"I've managed to break off some of this board but the rest is too strong and I can't break it. The ground is soft, though. I'm trying to dig some of it out with a rock. You're going to get a little dirty crawling out of there." Mindi's voice was strained.

"I don't care, just as long as I get out of here," I cried. I fought down a wave of panic and claustrophobia. I suddenly felt smothered by the darkness and the close quarters between the cages and the wall. I had trouble breathing. I closed my eyes and forced myself to continue my slow shuffle along the wall. To stay still would be to stay trapped.

Something grabbed my ankle. I screamed, and a few of the bears began grunting again in response.

"Shhhh! It's just me. Don't scream." It was Mindi.

I looked down. Like she said, one of the lower boards had been broken off and removed. Mindi's hand was stuck through the hole and held me by the ankle.

"Sorry, I thought you were going to go right by me," she apologized.

"I'm supposed to fit through that?" I screeched. The hole was impossibly small. That was the last straw. I lost the fight with hysteria and tears filled my eyes. Mindi's hand let go of my leg.

"It's okay. Calm down. It's bigger than it seems. We'll dig a bit more, too. You're skinny, you'll fit through. You'll see."

Mindi's confidence helped me calm down a bit. I bent over awkwardly in order to take a closer look. At that angle, I could see Mindi's face peering in and I blubbered a sob of relief.

"See, Sarah. It's almost big enough for you," Mindi was saying. "Just a bit more digging and you're a free woman."

I nodded and wiped away a stray tear. Together, we dug away with rocks and our fingers at the dirt floor underneath the broken board. Finally, as promised, the opening seemed big enough for me to fit through — barely. Freedom didn't come easily, though. I gritted my teeth as Mindi yanked me by the arms while I pushed against the bars of the cage behind me with my feet. I refused to cry out when the jagged, broken boards clawed at my skin and ripped my clothes as if unwilling to release me.

The whole time we struggled, I fought visions of razor-sharp bear claws swiping at my vulnerable legs as they suddenly slipped off the bars they were pushing against and landed at the angry bear's feet. But I continued to use the bars behind me as leverage; I was determined to force myself to get through that tiny opening no matter how much it hurt. I had to get out of there!

Finally, with one last aching wrench, I was free! I scrambled to my feet, threw my dirty arms around Mindi's neck, and hugged her tightly.

"Are you okay?" Mindi asked when I finally let her go. She examined my scratched arms and my filthy, torn clothes. "You look terrible. What are you going to say to your parents?"

"I don't care. I'm just glad I'm out of there," I said.

While I watched, Mindi propped the broken pieces of barn board back where they had once been attached in an attempt to hide the escape route. She pushed the loose dirt back into place and tried to pat it down so it looked undisturbed. Then, she took me by the arm and led me into the trees towards the hidden horses. As we walked, I told her about the bears.

"Why would Colin have a barn full of bears?" asked Mindi.

"I don't know," I said, shivering.

"And who were those men? Do you think they meant the bears when they were talking about his 'products'?"

"They must have been — that's all that was in there," I said.

"I don't understand this," said Mindi miserably. "Why would Colin want to sell bears? And who would want to buy them?"

Good questions. I decided not to tell her about the police file just then. She was upset enough, and besides, I wanted to be absolutely sure I knew what I was talking about before making accusations. I didn't know a thing about buying and selling bears. We jogged back to the horses in silence. In the stable, Mindi tried to help me clean up as much as possible. We traded T-shirts since mine was filthy.

By the time I managed to pedal my protesting body home, it was fully dark. Dad and Mom were at the door, apparently watching for me. Mom burst out of the house and ran down the driveway, the anger disappearing from her face when she saw the sad condition I was in.

"What happened?" she exploded. "Oh, I knew something was wrong when you didn't come home for supper!"

"I just fell off my bike into some prickly bushes," I told her. "I hurt my leg so I had trouble riding home. I guess I went a little too far. Sorry." I felt terrible lying, but at the time I didn't feel like I had much of a choice.

"Come inside, let's get you cleaned up, and you can tell us all about it. You must be starving." Mom put an arm around me, led me into the kitchen, and basically, you know, mothered me, while Dad scowled in the background, arms crossed, watching me get fussed over.

"You're up to something, I just know it," he said suddenly, shifting his weight and watching me closely.

I was expecting this, but Mom looked up, startled. "Oh, Ed. She fell off her bike, for goodness' sake! Stop treating your daughter like one of your criminals." She went back to examining my scratches and checking for broken bones. I pretended to be more hurt than I was and tried to appear extremely interested in Mom's findings. All the while, though, I was aware of Dad's penetrating stare through those narrowed eyes of his.

I couldn't look at him. He always knows when I'm lying.

You didn't say anything else after that, but it was obvious that you knew I was doing something I shouldn't have been. After all, that's when you made up that stupid rule that I wasn't allowed to go bike riding by myself anymore. I was supposed to think it was for safety reasons, since I seemed to be wiping out quite frequently, but I knew it was really so that Roy had to go with me and keep me out of trouble. Like a chaperon. How humiliating.

Anyway, for the record, I am sorry I didn't tell you the truth that night.

I really am.

Once I discovered those bears in Mr. Braemarie's barn, I was burning to figure out exactly why they were there. What purpose could Mr. Braemarie possibly have for keeping a bunch of bears secretly locked up in an old barn? It didn't make any sense. I decided I didn't know enough about bears, so some research was definitely needed. That week, I did lots of Internet surfing and learned some very disturbing things about bear poaching. I had no idea that certain bear parts were considered so valuable to some people ...

Page 1 of 3

ANIMALS IN THE WILD: BEARS

Jan/Feb — Volume VI, # 4

Poaching

Poaching is the illegal taking of wildlife outside of federal, provincial, or territorial hunting rules; the unlawful taking or killing of game.

Bear parts are in great demand internationally, especially in South Korea, China, and Japan. Bears are unique in that they are the only mammals that produce significant amounts of the bile tauro ursodeoxycholic acid (UDCA), which was listed as a medicine in the first official pharmacopeia in the world in China in 659 AD. Chinese medicine uses UDCA to treat an extensive list of ailments, from cancer to tooth decay. In spite of the fact that there are many synthetic and herbal alternatives to bear bile for medicinal purposes, genuine bile continues to be the preference of many.

Bear farms, in which bears are kept in restrictive cages and tapped for their bile, were initially established in China to ensure an ongoing supply of bear bile to a demanding market. Unfortunately, bear farming had the result of boosting demand for bear products, encouraging bear poaching. Bears who live in bear farms suffer psychological damage because of the living conditions. These farms are currently being regulated and phased out of existence.

Bear paw soup is considered an exotic delicacy by some. A bowl of this soup may sell for several hundred dollars. According to the Humane Society, in some Asian nations, bears, while still alive, have had their paws boiled or have been lowered onto hot coals and bludgeoned. There is a belief that the meat will be tastier when adrenaline is forced to flow through the animal during violent trauma before being killed. There have even been reports of bears being killed in front of restaurant customers.

Bear claws are desired for their ornamental value for traditional jewellery. Also, they are thought to be symbols of good health, strength, good luck, and fertility. In some countries, they are sold as souvenirs.

The shortages of the Asiatic black bear, sun bear, sloth bear, giant panda, and brown bear have led to increased black bear pressure throughout Canada and the U.S. In 1992, the Convention on International Trade in Endangered Species (CITES) listed the black bear in Appendix II as a species that is not considered threatened with extinction but that may become so if their trade is not regulated. Black bears are considered a "look-alike species" to those species actually threatened. This listing was to assist with the enforcement and protection of the endangered bear species. Since that date, a hunter wishing to transport any part of a black bear through Customs of any of the 152 nations that are signatories to CITES has to obtain a CITES export permit.

Many laws and regulations have been put in place to address the issue of black bear poaching in North America for the purposes of international black market trade. Conservation Officers are supplied with appropriate equipment and training. Special Investigation Units have been established through the Ministry of Natural Resources, and collaboration between Environment Canada Intelligence Officers and international enforcement agencies occurs to combat poaching operations.

Poachers are likely to work in groups. Approximately 60 percent of poachers are involved in other criminal activities: trafficking drugs; smuggling contraband; possession of prohibited weapons; break and enters; theft; and major traffic offences. There can be links to organized crime. Some work with sophisticated equipment, such as aircrafts, devices for night hunting, and scanners that allow them to eavesdrop on law enforcement communications.

Sentencing for poachers varies depending on the state or province in which the offences occur. Poachers may face imprisonment — up to six months for a first offence — and fines ranging from $6,000 to $50,000.

The next day at school, Mindi called me over to sit with her and her friends at lunch. To my surprise, I was even invited to join them for a sleepover that Friday night at Mindi's house. I couldn't believe Cori actually went along with it — she's not my biggest fan. And to my bigger surprise, when I asked if I could go that night at dinner, you actually let me without interrogating her mother first! Interesting how the rules were different for Mindi's home in town versus the farmhouse.

The point is that while at Mindi's, I learned something about Cori that would later turn out to be very important.

THE SLEEPOVER

DATE: FRIDAY, SEPTEMBER 21

LOCATION: MINDI'S HOUSE

It gave me a tremendous sense of freedom to not have to head to the bus area at the end of that day. Leaving the school with the other girls made me feel that I might have a chance to fit in here after all. My mood was soon dampened, however, because of Cori. She clearly wasn't thrilled to have me along. She didn't talk to me once during the short walk to Mindi's. She deliberately ignored me while we were making snacks. Then she acted like I wasn't even there when we sat in the TV room to watch *Oprah* while we ate. It was very obvious; I wasn't welcome.

When Stacey and Mindi took our used cups and bowls back to the kitchen, Cori and I were stuck alone together. The awkward silence between us was unbearable — for me, anyway, as she didn't look like she cared. When I couldn't stand sitting there in silence any longer, I mumbled something about helping out in the kitchen and escaped from the room. How can anybody be so unfriendly? As I approached the kitchen, I heard Mindi speaking.

"We have to do something about Cori. She's being awful to Sarah. She's going to ruin everybody's fun."

I gulped and froze in my tracks.

"I know," Stacey agreed. "Maybe you shouldn't have invited Sarah. For some reason, Cori doesn't really like her."

"What do you mean I shouldn't have invited Sarah? She's my friend and I have every right to invite any friend I want to my house. Besides, it isn't Sarah who's ruining our fun. It's Cori. We have to talk to her."

My face burned and I blinked back a tear, silently thanking Mindi for calling me her friend.

"I'll talk to Cori," said Stacey. "I'll take care of this."

I wanted to die. Why didn't I just go home on the bus, as usual? Not knowing what else to do, I reluctantly walked back to the TV room. As I entered, Cori threw me a dirty look. That did it! Now, I was angry. How dare she be so rude to me? Who did she think she was? I was Mindi's friend; she said so herself.

Before I could actually say anything, Stacey and Mindi came into the room behind me, causing a magical transformation in Cori's face. She went from totally hostile to ultra-friendly. What a fake.

"We had a great idea, you guys!" Mindi announced brightly — a little too brightly. "Let's grab a basketball and head over to the school and play two-on-two before supper! There's usually lots of guys hanging around there," she added, smiling hopefully.

"Sounds good to me, Mindi," chimed in Stacey, mechanically, as if the lines had been rehearsed. "What do you think, guys? Sound good?"

Cori shrugged nonchalantly, but she did get up. I forced myself to smile, and I mean *forced*, while secretly aching inside. It was just too painful. I felt like a charity case. I knew that I was the cause of all this awkwardness.

"Actually," I said, stiffly, "I think I'm going to head out. There's something I forgot I have to do at home tonight. Could I use your phone, Mindi?"

Mindi eyes widened in alarm. "No, you can't, Sarah. I want you to stay!" she protested. "We'll play basketball and have a great time, you'll see."

"We want you to stay, Sarah," chimed in Stacey. "Really we do." She looked hard at Cori. Cori was smirking, finally enjoying herself.

Mindi tightly linked her arm through mine. "We need you to stay so we can play two-on-two, right, guys?" She looked hard at Cori, who had no choice but to grudgingly agree.

I looked back and forth between Mindi and Stacey. They were trying so hard to make this fun. I decided that I should at least hang around to play a little basketball, then I'd definitely go home. So I grudgingly agreed to stay a bit longer.

During the short walk to the school, Mindi and I walked ahead of Stacey and Cori. I didn't have to look behind us to know that Stacey was earnestly appealing to Cori to be nice to me. How humiliating. My face burned the whole way to school. I wasn't used to feeling like such an outsider, like an intruder into other people's lives, and I hated every minute of it.

Dad, I bet you didn't realize how cruel teenage girls could be to each other, did you? See what your stupid transfer was putting me through? We should have just stayed in Mississauga where I actually had friends who liked having me around.

"I really have to go home after this, Mindi. Sorry," I said, trying hard to keep the tremor out of my voice.

"No, Sarah!" Mindi pleaded. "Stacey and I want you to stay. Let's just have fun."

"Mindi, nobody's having fun. Cori doesn't like me and that's that. You can't please everyone," I shrugged, turning my face away from Mindi so she wouldn't see me blinking back tears. The last thing I needed was for my so-called new friends to know how upsetting all this was to me, how desperately I wanted to fit in with them and belong.

"Cori just has to get to know you. Then she'll like you as much as Stacey and I do, you'll see," Mindi reassured me. "Please don't go home."

I smiled weakly but didn't answer. Mindi was wrong. I didn't think Cori would ever like me.

As Stacey predicted, there were boys hanging around the outdoor basketball courts at school. Chris LeBlanc, one of Roy's new friends, was among them. He was busy talking to some other boys using wide gestures with his arms, reminding me of Roy's dramatics. He turned when we approached, smiled, and waved. We waved back, myself included. I hoped he didn't remember me and Roy's goofy story about my surgery.

"Hi, Chris. Watcha doing?" Cori called brightly.

Wouldn't you know it? Cori the grouch-queen undergoes yet another magical transformation at the sight of the opposite sex. Bitter, unattractive frowns instantaneously disappear, to be replaced by wide, toothy smiles. Not only is she a fake, she's a flirt. A regular Dr. Jekyll and Miss Hyde.

"Hi, Cori. Just hanging out. We were about to start a game. Why don't you girls join in? That would give us enough for two full teams."

Cori and I ended up on the same team, but the new and improved Cori didn't seem to mind my presence one bit. In fact, she was real buddy-buddy with me in front of the guys. What an actress!

Playing with the older boys made for a fast-paced, physical game. It didn't help that every time I got the ball, Chris was right there guarding me, making it just about impossible to pass or shoot. He was good. In the end, my team won. Even Cori gave me a high-five.

I glanced back at the basketball court as we began the return walk to Mindi's. Chris was watching us go and he gave me a small wave. I returned it.

"Are you two in love or what, girl?" Stacey laughed.

"What do you mean?" I asked, shocked.

"Are you kidding? You and Chris! He was all over you the whole game!" Stacey accused with glee.

"He was *guarding* me. He's *supposed* to be all over me," I protested.

"Yeah — but he was *all over you*!" repeated Stacey.

"He's just a good basketball player," I said with a shrug.

This caused such an eruption of giggles from the others that I couldn't help but join in. What the heck, if they wanted to think that Chris and I had something going on, let them.

Don't have a hairy canary, Dad, we didn't.

"You can have Chris," said Cori, who seemed to have given up entirely on scowling, even with no boys around. "It's Ryan for me!"

"Oh, was he the one with the dark hair and the Nike shirt?" I asked.

"Yes! He's to die for!" breathed Cori, spinning around.

"We all want him!" chimed in Stacey.

"Except Sarah," noted Mindi. "She's already got Chris!"

I blushed like crazy but I was happy. We were finally all getting along. I ended up staying the night after all. What the heck, I was actually having some fun. Cori and I seemed to have come to a truce. We'd never be best friends, but we could get along. Go figure.

After supper, we did the usual sleepover stuff. You know, put on lots of makeup, played with each other's hair (mine ended up full of tiny braids), did our nails, and so on and so forth. Amazingly, Cori continued to be civil to me, even friendly at times, when she forgot that she wasn't supposed to like me. Afterwards, we made popcorn and settled down to watch a movie that Mindi's mom had rented for us. The movie was a love story with lots of romance and adventure. It was cool. When it was over, we talked about how romantic it would be to fall in love with a prince and live happily ever after.

"What about Roy?" asked Cori with a sideways glance at me. "Who thinks *he'd* make a good prince?"

"Yuck! I think I'm going to puke!" I yelled. I rolled around on the floor, holding my hands to my throat and sticking out my tongue. Like I said, I was actually having a good time. Besides, any time I get to trash Roy is a good time.

"I'm sure Mindi's thinking of Roy," pointed out Stacey. Mindi giggled.

I sat up, ready to stop this train of thought once and for all. I leaned towards them and lowered my voice confidentially. "You think Roy's hot?" I asked them.

"Yeah," nodded Stacey. The others nodded right along with her, causing the gorge to rise up in my throat again.

"See, you think you like Roy but that's because you don't know him," I said. "I could tell you things about him that would make your toes curl."

"Really? Tell us!" said Cori, eagerly.

That was not the reaction I was going for.

"No," I protested. "I meant toes curling in a bad way. I can tell you bad things about Roy. Things that would make you hate him."

"You couldn't tell me anything to make me hate Roy," said Mindi with a dreamy look on her face.

Ugh! Clearly I had no control over these girls. If they wanted to think Roy's a hottie, I guess I wasn't going to be able to convince them otherwise. They'd just have to find out for themselves what a pig he really was. They talked a bit longer about Roy but I tuned them out. I couldn't take it anymore.

"Sarah, did you know that Cori's dad is a Conservation Officer?" asked Mindi. I was startled out of my reverie by this abrupt change in topic.

"Oh, yeah?" I said, looking up from the toenail I'd been picking at.

"Well, weren't you telling me that you have a project to do for one of your classes that has to do with wildlife or something?" she asked, raising her eyebrows as if urging me to go along with her story.

"Right. My project. I forgot all about it," I said, slapping my forehead. "How could I forget?" Clearly, Mindi was not prepared to tell her friends about the occupants of Mr. Braemarie's barn. I felt special, knowing that I shared this secret with her.

"Maybe you could talk to Cori's dad and ask him some questions to help you with your project," suggested Mindi. "What do you think, Cori, would your dad mind?"

Cori frowned. I'm sure it was killing her to think about doing something nice for me. "I guess he wouldn't mind." She looked at me. "He's pretty busy, though, I don't know when he'd get a chance to see you."

"Maybe Sarah and I can go over to your house one day next week and Sarah could talk to him then. Does he have any books we could borrow?" persisted Mindi.

I stared at her. Did she have this planned? If so, it would have been nice if she'd filled me in.

"Yeah sure," shrugged Cori. "He has books and videos. Tons of them. What exactly do you want information about, Sarah?"

"I have to do my project about bears and poachers," I said, with a sideways glance at Mindi. She flinched slightly at "poachers." I hadn't had a chance to share any of the research I'd done with her so we hadn't talked yet about the likelihood of Mr. Braemarie being a poacher. I thought it was very likely. How else would you explain the bears locked in his barn?

"I'll look at home tomorrow and see what he has," she said.

"Thanks."

I watched Cori toss back her blonde hair as the topic changed back to boys and thought that maybe, just maybe, Cori wasn't so bad after all. She seemed to be willing to help me with what she thought was a school project. And maybe she'd even invite me over, like Mindi suggested, and I'd be able to ask her dad, the Conservation Officer, some questions about bears and poaching. It sure would be easier than trying to get information from the Internet.

I was glad I decided to stay.

So that's how Mindi found out that I suspected Mr. Braemarie was a poacher. I was certain that his barn was a bear farm — just like the ones I read about in China. What other explanation made sense? Those bears must be getting tapped for their bile. Of course, I had no idea what tapping for bile looked like, but I was sure that was what was going on.

I was disappointed on Monday when Cori told me she forgot to check at home for books or videos about bears and poaching. Then on Tuesday, I was disappointed further to learn that she hadn't even mentioned me to her father. Finally, by Wednesday, it was clear that Cori had no intention of helping me out in the least with my "project." How could I have thought that she might be a decent person after all? My first impressions, apparently, were accurate.

So, feeling like Mindi and I were doing nothing and going nowhere, while bears were waiting to be sold and slaughtered right in front of our eyes, I decided to invite myself over to the farmhouse that day after school. I needed to talk to Mindi, away from Cori and Stacey. Talking on the bus never worked since Mindi was always too busy flirting with Roy for us to have a decent conversation. We had to figure out what to do about those bears. I couldn't just sit around and do nothing!

I wasn't planning to go anywhere near the barn again. Honestly.

A Doorway

Date: Wednesday, September 26

Location: The Farmhouse

I tried to leave the house without Roy, but Mom caught me and, heeding Dad's new rule, made him go with me. He wasn't too happy about it either, especially when he found out where I was going.

"How fair is this?" he ranted as we biked towards Mindi's house. "You mess up, and now I'm the one who's stuck babysitting."

"Do you think I like this?" I retorted. "When we get to Mindi's, why don't you do me a favour and take an extra-long ride down the road. I only need to talk to her for a few minutes. Then we'll go straight home, I promise."

He grunted at me. "Now she's giving me orders," he said to the sky. We pedalled in silence for a while.

"Okay, I'll give you fifteen minutes, tops," he finally agreed. "I'll wait for you at the mailbox."

Roy pouted the rest of the way there, allowing me time to think about Mr. Braemarie and his bears. For the millionth time, I wished I'd had a chance to read Dad's file with his name on it. Darn meddling Roy! What exactly did the police have on Mr. Braemarie? I was dying to know.

Soon, I was swinging into Mindi's driveway. Roy, keeping to his word, kept pedalling, giving me the time I needed with Mindi.

"Fifteen minutes and I'm back at the mailbox!" he shouted over his shoulder.

I took the porch steps two at a time and knocked on the door. No answer. I knocked again. No answer. I looked back at the driveway. No car. Apparently, nobody was home. But I watched Mindi get off the bus, and she said she'd wait for me on the porch! I was confused. Dejected, I started to turn back to my bike, but my feet unexpectedly developed a will of their own. They moved of their own accord past my bike and towards the old barn.

I called out Mindi's name as if looking for her, just in case someone was around after all. However, I heard nothing but my own shallow breathing. I picked up the pace and kept calling. Nothing. The place was deserted. At the barn, I continued to call Mindi's name. Still no answer. The place was totally deserted.

What luck! What an opportunity!

I came to the spot where Mindi had hauled me out to freedom. She had done a pretty good job covering up the hole we had made. In fact, I almost walked right by it. I hunkered down and gently pulled the broken boards loose again. They came away easily. I stared in amazement. To think that I actually fit through such a small space. No wonder I got all scratched up! I idly touched the scrapes on my arms as I leaned in and examined the area around the removed board. Some of the surrounding boards seemed a bit rotten too. I tugged at them, but they were more sturdy than they looked.

I knew that I needed to get back in that barn more than anything in the world, even if those bears were a bit freaky. Some things were too important not to do, and I had to see if the bears were being tapped for bile like at the bear farms in China I read about. If I could only make the hole a bit bigger, then I could get in and back out without getting all scraped up again. Suddenly, I knew what I had to do. I ran across the field to the stable. There I found, right in its proper place, the pitchfork that was used to clean out the horses' stalls.

Back at the barn, I wedged the prongs of the pitchfork into the vertical gap between the remaining barn boards, creating a lever. Carefully, I pushed on the pitchfork's handle, using the curve of the fork as a fulcrum. All those boring science classes about simple machines were coming in handy after all. I pushed harder — tentatively. The board didn't move. I tried again, with real force, and this time I heard the wood splintering. I pushed again, throwing my body into it, grunting with the effort. Suddenly, the board gave with a mighty crack and I fell against the barn wall with the pitchfork handle still clutched tightly in my hands. The board now hung loosely, still stubbornly attached to the wall. I looked at it and smiled. It was worth the bump on the head and the scraped knuckles.

I tugged and tugged at the loose board. I finally gave a mighty heave and the board cracked, causing me to lose my balance and fall backwards into the dirt, the board still gripped tightly in my hands. I quickly scrambled to my knees and stuck my head inside the bigger hole I had just created. I was staring at the bars of a cage about an arm's length away. Through them, I could see the shining brown eyes and glistening snout of a bear leaning down toward me, his hot breath warming my face.

"Whoa, big bear," I said, taken aback. "Sorry to disturb you."

Hurriedly, I pulled my head out and carefully replaced the boards. I cleaned up the splinters of wood that were lying about on the ground and stood back to admire my work. Unless you knew what you were looking for, you could once again barely tell that the barn had been tampered with.

The sound of a car wiped the smile off my face. The engine noise abruptly stopped and door slams echoed ominously in my head. My heart leaped into my throat. Running as fast as my legs could go, I dashed back towards the stable to return the pitchfork. No sooner had I hung up the tool than Mindi walked into the barn, calling my name.

"Sarah! Are you here?"

I jumped at her voice. "Yeah, I'm here. I was looking for you and figured this is where you'd be." I wasn't quite ready to tell her about the renovations I had made to the barn.

"Sorry I wasn't here when you got here," continued Mindi, "but Colin and Mom were all excited about some beaver dam they discovered this morning while they were hiking, and they just had to show it to me. We were taking forever looking at this stupid dam, until I told them you were coming over. Well, you should have seen Colin move then. He practically shoved us both into the car and he sped all the way home. I guess he didn't like the idea of you here waiting for me all by yourself."

"I guess not." I nodded. Of course he wouldn't want anyone here by themselves, I thought. They might make some discoveries. He had things to hide.

"We saw your brother on the drive home," said Mindi, changing the topic.

"Oh yeah?"

"He was biking this way. You should ask him to come over with you sometime," she suggested with a shy smile.

"That might happen sooner than you think," I mumbled.

"What's that?"

"Never mind. Look, I only have a few minutes and I need to talk to you about the bears and the research I've been doing."

Her face darkened, the smile gone. She didn't look too keen to listen, but I talked anyway. This wasn't going to go away. I described what I learned about bears and poaching. I was in the middle of explaining how bear farms worked when Mr. Braemarie appeared out of nowhere.

"So you were in here, were you?" His big voice boomed, filling the stable.

I stopped talking in mid-sentence and swung around, startled. "Yes, sir. I thought Mindi would be waiting for me in here when she wasn't up at the house," I explained, trying to keep the tremor out of my voice. It always did that when I lied. Very annoying.

"Humph," he grunted, staring at me until I was forced to look away. "There's a young man waiting in our driveway looking for you."

"That would be Roy, my brother," I hurriedly explained, wiping my sweaty palms on my jeans. "Uh, he was curious about your horses. I told him not to come and be a pest, but you know brothers." It sounded like such a lame explanation but it seemed to work.

"Everybody loves horses," said Mr. Braemarie, nodding. "Mindi, why don't you go get him?"

Mindi's face lit up like a Christmas tree as she rushed away to get Roy. No sooner had she left the barn than Mr. Braemarie stepped closer to me. The smile had dissolved off his face.

"You know, Sarah," he said. He tilted his head and fixed his penetrating gaze on me. "I have a problem with people coming onto my property when I'm not here." He held up his hand to stop my apology. "I know Mindi asked you to meet her, but next time you come here and we're not here, if there is a next time, wait at the house or go home."

I nodded, speechless.

He continued to stare at me. He leaned closer and lowered his voice to a growl.

"You came straight to the stable to look for Mindi, did you?"

I nodded again and croaked, "Y-y-yes."

"You're sure about that?" He raised his eyebrows and shrugged. "You didn't happen to look anywhere else for Mindi while you were here — alone?"

I gulped. "No. I was only here ... after I knocked at the house. This is where I thought Mindi would be. I was just starting to wonder if I'd made a mistake about what time I was supposed to meet her when she showed up." I tried a weak smile but I couldn't quite pull it off.

Mr. Braemarie's eyes narrowed and he pointed at me. "Just as long as you weren't snooping around. People can get hurt by snooping around other people's property, you know."

I stepped back, shaking my head vigorously. "No, sir. I wouldn't snoop around," I assured him.

"Good. I sure wouldn't want to see you get hurt." He glared at me again as if he really would want to see it. Then, just as abruptly as he arrived, he turned and strode out of the stable.

I sagged against the wall. I couldn't believe it. Mr. Braemarie had just threatened me. I had just been threatened!

I was still sagging when Mindi returned with Roy. They didn't even look my way. There I was, absolutely limp with fear, so that I couldn't even move, and they didn't bother to notice. Mindi was far too busy giving Roy the grand tour, introducing him to each of the horses, just like she did with me not too long ago. I might as well have been a fly on Candy's back for the attention I got. It was annoying. And sickening. Not only was Mindi giggling and flirting like crazy with

Roy, but he seemed to be enjoying every minute of it. This could only happen to me. There I was, crushed and terrified after receiving a death threat from a crazed, violent poacher, and there they were acting like they were on a date!

I finally gave up waiting for them to ask me what was wrong and pushed myself off the wall. On the bright side, Roy wasn't dragging me home. My fifteen minutes were over ages ago, yet he didn't seem to care. I began to saddle up Ginger, hoping like crazy that I was doing it right so that Roy would be put in his place. Me — knowledgeable horse person. Him — unwelcome intruder. Mindi offered to let him ride Candy, but with a sideways glance at me, he declined. Chicken. Thunder was too difficult for a beginner to ride, so after Mindi batted her eyes a few more times, Roy agreed to wait around while I had a quick lesson on Ginger.

Mindi and I were quiet at first, as we rode the horses single file into the fenced field. I closed my eyes and drank in the fresh country air. Me! A city girl! I had to admit, I was really beginning to appreciate the beauty of the outdoors in the country. The horses, the freshness of the air, the smell of the trees, and my new friend Mindi all made me feel so content that I could almost forget about my close encounter with Mr. Braemarie. Riding a horse on a beautiful fall afternoon was definitely not something I'd ever get to do in Mississauga.

Mindi had her horse trot around the perimeter of the fence while Roy leaned with one foot on the lower fence rail and looked on. She beckoned for me to follow, which I was thrilled to be able to do. After a few rounds of this, we slowed to a walk. Mindi brought her horse alongside mine.

Her face was grim. "So, do you think that's what Colin is doing — bear poaching? Running a bear farm?" she asked quietly, picking up our previous conversation as if no time had elapsed.

"I'm not totally sure yet." I looked over at Roy. He was now perched on the fence blowing on a blade of grass to make it whistle; he couldn't hear us.

"I didn't go straight to the stable to wait for you today," I confided.

Mindi frowned. "No?"

I explained. I told her all about our new and improved barn doorway. I also told her how I needed to get back into the barn to look more closely at the bears, to see if they were being tapped for bile.

"What would we look for?" she asked with wide eyes.

I shrugged. "Anything unusual, I guess. Machinery, tubes. I don't really know. Oh, and I don't think Mr. Braemarie likes me being here," I continued. I told her how he threatened me while she was getting Roy.

I looked at Mindi's downcast face and suddenly remembered that this was her mom's boyfriend we were talking about. Also, the owner of these wonderful horses that Mindi loved so much. And I call Roy insensitive.

"I'm sorry," I stammered. "I know this is hard for you to hear."

"I just can't believe it." Mindi shook her head. "I mean, my mom really likes this guy." Her big eyes searched mine. "I like him, too. This is going to ruin everything." She blinked back tears. "I can't believe this is happening. I thought Colin was such a nice guy, but then he slammed a door in my face, you saw him with a gun in the barn, then we found out he lied about the farm machinery, and now you tell me that he threatened you. I don't know what to think anymore! I don't know what to do! Maybe I should just stay at home and forget about all this!"

I felt terrible that I'd upset Mindi so much. I put my hand on her shoulder. "We can't forget about it, we need to find out if I'm wrong," I said. "In fact, I probably am wrong. Why don't we do some investigating to clear Mr. Braemarie's name — you and me. Okay? Partners?"

Mindi gave me a pathetic smile. "Right. Partners. We need to figure out what's going on here. Maybe I just need to go in the barn for myself and see what's in there, and now you've got a little doorway all ready for us."

"That's the spirit, partner," I said, grinning. And as I looked at her stricken face, I really hoped that I was wrong about Mr. Braemarie. But in my heart, I was already sure that I was right.

On the way home, Roy demanded to know what I'd said to Mindi in the field to make her so upset. He wouldn't let up until I finally gave in and told him about the bears in the barn and the research I'd done, making me think that Mr. Braemarie was operating a bear farm. I left out how Mr. Braemarie had threatened me — no need to give him more of a reason to hit the panic button, he was close enough to it as it was.

It took a lot of arguing, pleading, and bribing to stop Roy from going straight to you, Dad, right then and there with the whole story. But the thought of possibly falsely accus-

ing Mr. Braemarie, a close friend of Mindi and her mom, finally kept him quiet. Instead, he decided he'd just keep escorting me to the farmhouse whenever I insisted on going. This was supposed to keep me out of trouble. Personally, I think he just wanted to spend more time with Mindi.

That night at home, I decided that the research I'd done so far didn't give me enough local information. I needed to know if poaching was a problem here in Muskoka. I had to talk to Mr. Stedman. As a local Conservation Officer, he'd know about local poaching concerns. Roy seemed to agree, for whatever that's worth.

I phoned Cori's house. It was the hardest phone number I've ever had to punch in. It was bad enough having to look at her pinched, sour face scowling at me every time I asked her if she remembered to bring me one of her dad's books, but to actually phone her ... ugh! But I had to do it. I needed to speak to her father.

She picked up on the first ring. She probably had call display and thought Roy was phoning to ask her out. She's that conceited.

"Hello."

"Hi, Cori, it's Sarah."

"Oh." She wasn't successful at keeping the disappointment out of her voice. I took a fortifying breath.

"I was wondering if it would be possible to speak to your dad for a minute. You know, about my project," I said, going right to the point. There was no need to make small talk, I figured. Neither one of us wanted me to.

"He's not here," she said sharply. "I told you, he's very busy."

"But it's eight o'clock at night," I argued. "I thought he'd be home by now."

"Well, he isn't," she said.

"Do you mind asking him to call me when he gets home?" I asked, trying my best to keep my voice polite when all I wanted to do was yell at her.

A heavy sigh.

"Look, Sarah," she said, her voice low, "why don't we just be straight with each other here? I'm not about to bother my dad about your stupid little project. He's busy. Do your own research."

Then she hung up, but not before I heard her dad yelling in the background, asking who was calling.

I sat there, stunned, and stared at the phone in my hand until it began the loud beeping noise to let me know it was off the hook. I had no idea she'd be that rude. How could Mindi be friends with this nasty person? I sighed. It was just an obstacle I'd have to work around. I got right to work. Half an hour later, I was still at it. I sat cross-legged on my bed, the Muskoka and Surrounding Areas telephone book splayed open on my lap. My face was hot, my temper fiery. Roy popped his head into my room — without knocking, as usual.

"Did you call yet?" he whispered.

"Yeah, I called," I sputtered. "Wait till you hear this."

He stepped into my room and closed the door behind him. I told him about my close encounter with Cori. He shook his head in disbelief.

"Wow," he said and whistled. "She's always been so sweet to me."

I snorted.

"I don't need her help. I'm going to make an appointment with her dad myself but I can't figure out which number to call."

I held up the phone book, and he stared at it. I hated asking for his help like that, but I was getting desperate. I had been through the government section of the phone book umpteen times and I couldn't figure out which number to call in order to speak to a Conservation Officer. Why couldn't they just list "Conservation Officers" in the yellow pages? That would have made my life a lot easier.

"Did you look under Ministry of Natural Resources?" asked Roy.

"No, I looked under hairstylists," I retorted.

"Do you want my help or not?"

"Yes," I sighed.

Roy sat on the edge of my bed and took the proffered book. His brow furrowed as he scanned the pages. "You're in the federal and provincial section. Let's try looking under municipal government." I scowled. I hated when he knew more about something than I did. But what could I say? I'd asked for his help.

Roy continued searching through the book. Finally he looked up. "Why don't you just try calling the municipal office in Bracebridge and whoever is there should be able to give you a number to call."

"Okay, what's the number for the municipal office?" I reached for the phone lying on my bed.

"Nobody will be there now, goof. It's after office hours. You'll have to phone in the morning from school." He handed back the phone book, holding his finger on the number I wanted. I took it and wrote the number down in my notebook.

Roy stood up.

"Thanks." I smiled up at him.

He smiled back.

It was a rare, touching moment.

That Friday morning, I was a nervous wreck. I spilled orange juice all over the kitchen table and burned my toast while I was cleaning it up. You see, not only was it the day we were to find out who made the final cuts for the school basketball team, but Mindi and I were also scheduled to meet with Mr. Stedman at the Municipal Building in town over the lunch hour. No thanks to Cori. We scraped together every last penny we had to pay for the cab ride since there were no public buses running here in the sticks.

Just think, when I'm a real detective, I'll have an expense account!

Mr. Stedman

Date: Friday, September 28

Location: School and the Ministry Offices

Between first and second periods that morning, I rushed to the crowded gym where the final basketball team list was posted. I met Mindi, Stacey, and Cori there. Cori and I exchanged a nasty look behind Mindi and Stacey's backs. That was our usual greeting now. Neither of us mentioned to the others about our phone conversation, and it looked like it was going to be our little secret.

I hung back and watched nervously as some girls walked away from the posting with smiles, some with tears. My heart was fluttering. How would I be walking away? Now that I had rushed there, eager to find out if I made the team, I found I didn't have the courage to step into the crowd and actually check the list. The basketball court was the only place I really felt like I belonged so far at this school; I knew I'd die if my name wasn't on that list.

To make things worse, there was a crowd of boys standing around enjoying the show. Among the crowd were, of course, Roy and his friends. Roy always had to be where the action was. I quickly turned my back on them, hoping Roy hadn't seen me, but I was too late. I was suddenly being pushed forward into the crowd by someone who had grabbed my arm from behind. Guess who?

"Come on, Sarah, don't be shy. Let's see if you made the team," announced Roy loudly. Heads turned with interest at his voice. Just like he wanted.

"Get lost, Roy!" I hissed, trying to squirm out of his grip. "Leave me alone."

"Are you nervous? Do you want me to look for you?" he asked in mock concern. He let go of my arm and made a show of backing away from me with trembling legs and chattering teeth. My eyes pleaded with him to stop, but he was beyond stopping. He had his audience and he could be a real jerk.

Roy squeezed his way through the crowd of girls, saying, "Excuse me ladies, stud coming through. Pardon me."

To my disgust, the girls giggled and made room for him. How sickening. I was just about to hurl when Roy's booming voice demanded everyone's full attention once again.

"Well, let's see here," he said. I held my breath as his finger moved slowly down the list of names.

"Well, look at that, Cori Stedman," he announced with a wave of his hand. Cori squealed with delight. Mindi and Stacey gave her high-fives. I did my best to paste a huge smile on my face and pretend that Roy's stupid little game didn't bother me at all.

Roy continued his search down the list of names. Suddenly, his hands flew to his face and he exclaimed in a really pathetic Southern accent, "Oh, I do declare! There's Mindi Roberts." Mindi grinned from ear to ear as she took her high-fives from us; I joined in this time. Roy was really hamming it up now; like I've said, he loves being the centre of attention. Right then, he was in his glory.

"Yup, and here's Stacey Payton," he called out, his finger near the bottom of the list. I tried my best to keep that foolish grin on my face, but my heart felt like it was in a steel trap as I watched Roy's finger run slowly down the rest of the list. Then his finger ran out of names. My worst fear was coming true. He turned slowly to me, looking truly sad, and shrugged.

"Sorry, kid, not this year," he said.

I told myself I wasn't surprised, that I knew I wasn't going to make the team. I didn't let that stupid grin waver from my face in spite of the cold steel vice that was squeezing my heart.

"I guess I'm just going to have to practise up for next year's tryouts," I said, struggling to keep the tremor out of my voice. Roy stared at me. The corners of his lips began to twitch.

"Naahhhh, I'm just kidding! There's your name right there!" he exploded, pointing his finger to a name that was near the top of the list. He broke out into gales of laughter. "Gotcha!"

The steel vice around my heart sprang open and I began to breathe again. I received my high-fives with enthusiasm amongst laughter and grins from the others. When Roy tried to join in, I gave him a hard shove.

"You idiot!" I may have been laughing in front of the others, but inside, I vowed to find a way to get back at him for that humiliating scene.

Cori, the little actress, pretended that she sympathized with me. She gave Roy a bunch of little playful shoves and said, "That was mean, Roy!" and, "You're bad, Roy!" while her eyes twinkled with merriment. Not only was she an actress, she was a very bad one.

Roy doubled over in laughter again. "You should have seen your face, Sarah." He straightened himself up. "I'll just have to practise more," he said, his voice high-pitched, his chin and lip trembling in a really bad imitation of me, which, of course, set him off laughing like a hyena again. What a moron.

"Yeah, great. Everyone thinks you're Mr. Funny Man now, Roy," I shot back.

"Aw, I wouldn't have done it if I didn't already know you'd made the team," he protested. He turned to Mindi and his eyebrows arched high over a puppy-dog face. "I'm not *that* mean," he said, giving his eyebrows a little wiggle. Mindi rewarded him with a giggle. I scowled.

"C'mon, guys. Let's blow," he said finally, walking out of the gym. "Let's go find somebody with a sense of humour."

I was glad to see his back, but I hated the look of disappointment on Mindi's face. What did she see in that show-off, anyway? And why does he always try to ruin my life?

* * *

Mindi and I practically sprinted out of our second-period class. A cab was waiting for us. We had an hour before third period began after lunch. We figured it would take us at least ten minutes to get to the Ministry offices where we had arranged to meet Mr. Stedman. We wanted to have as much time as possible with him before we had to head back to school. We arrived right on time, and I immediately told the receptionist we had an appointment. She motioned for us to sit down.

"You do all the talking, okay?" whispered Mindi. This was at least the fourth time she'd said that to me. "Remember, we're not going to say anything about Colin's barn, right?"

"Don't worry, he's just going to think we're working on a school project," I reminded her. "Besides, we don't really know what Mr. Braemarie's doing with those bears so we shouldn't say anything."

"Right," agreed Mindi. "We don't want to cause him any trouble when he's not even doing anything wrong."

I nodded to Mindi but wondered, *What could he be doing right with a bunch of bears locked up in an old barn?*

We weren't kept waiting long. Soon, a man about the same height as me came out to the reception area and said a friendly hello to Mindi. Mindi then introduced him to me as Mr. Stedman. What he lacked in height, he made up in muscle. His shirt sleeves were rolled up to reveal some bulging biceps. He shook our hands then led us to his small office.

"So, I didn't realize that you'd be coming along with Sarah, Mindi. Nice to see you again," said Mr. Stedman.

Mindi smiled. "I just thought I'd tag along to keep Sarah company."

"Ah, you're being a good friend," he said, nodding.

Mr. Stedman was in uniform. Khaki pants with a matching shirt, plenty of pockets. He wore a patch on his left sleeve indicating his station. His wide-brimmed hat was sitting on the corner of his desk. A worn leather briefcase on the floor leaned against the desk, unable to stand on its own anymore.

"Have a seat, ladies," he said, taking his place behind the desk. "I have to tell you, I don't get a chance to meet with young people very often. Not because I don't want to, I just don't get asked to. I think it's terrific that you want to know more about wildlife here in Muskoka. It's for a school project, did you say?"

"Yes, it is," I began. "Maybe Cori mentioned something about it to you?"

He looked puzzled. "No, she hasn't mentioned anything."

I shrugged and exchanged a look with Mindi, as if to say, See? What did I tell you about that girl?

"It doesn't matter," said Mindi. "We just wondered if she said something, since you're a Conservation Officer and the project is about wildlife."

"Yes, and I already did some research, Mr. Stedman," I added, "on the Internet, but I couldn't find any local information for my project."

"Okay," he said, leaning back in his chair. "Is there a specific kind of wildlife you're focusing on?"

Mindi looked at me. I cleared my throat.

"Well, we're mainly focusing on bears," I began.

"Bears. Okay then, I can give you information about the prevalence of black bears in North America, their appearance, breeding habits, their young, enemies … whatever you want to know. I have some pamphlets here that are quite good …" Mr. Stedman turned and rummaged through some piles of papers on the ledge behind him. He swung back holding out two pamphlets about black bears. I took them with a thank you.

He then proceeded to tell us all he knew about bears. And believe me, he knew a lot. At first I was very interested, and dutifully took notes, but as time went on and he was still talking, I had to fake my interest. Then I couldn't even do that anymore. It was just too boring. I started fidgeting in my seat and glancing at my watch. How did I lose control of this interview? We'd have to leave soon in order to get back to school in time for third period. I kept waiting for a break in his incredibly long monologue so I could jump in and get to the real reason we were there; I thought it would be rude to interrupt him. Finally he took a breath.

"How much of a problem is poaching here in Muskoka?" I asked quickly, before he could start talking again.

"Poaching?" Mr. Stedman frowned. "Ugly subject. You don't really want to get into that, do you?"

I smiled at him. "I came across some information on the Internet about the demand for bear parts and how much of a growing problem bear poaching is becoming in Canada. So I want to include that information in my project. How much poaching goes on around here, Mr. Stedman?" I asked.

He gave a harsh laugh and clasped his hands on the table. "Oh, there's the odd guy who shoots a bear or two out of season because the bear's become a nuisance. You know, the usual, hanging around, getting into the garbage and so on." Mr. Stedman's clasped hands whitened at the knuckles as he spoke. "No, Muskoka's pretty tame when it comes to big business poaching of the kind you would have read about on the Internet."

"But, Mr. Stedman, I read that most poaching happens where the bear population is the highest and the human population is low. Wouldn't that describe Muskoka?" I asked.

He laughed. "We're not that desolate out here."

"What happens to people who are caught poaching bears?" asked Mindi, breaking her own rule about me doing all the talking.

"Well, now. That would be up to the court system. It's against the law to possess, for instance, a black bear gall, under Section 50 of the Ontario Fish and Wildlife Conservation Act. And it is also against the law to export bear parts under the Wild Animal and Plant Protection and Regulation of International and Interprovincial Trade Act. Also, bears are protected by the Convention on the International Trade of Endangered Species of Wild Fauna and Flora. Usually, someone caught poaching and breaking those laws would be given a pretty hefty fine, possibly even some jail time."

"What about people who keep bears as pets?" Mindi asked. "Is that allowed?"

He frowned. "I don't know of anybody who'd want to keep a bear for a pet. They're wild animals." He paused, then said, "There are restrictions in place for any exotic pets. Are you talking about someone you know?"

"No," Mindi said quickly, her face reddening slightly. "Just wondering if that ever happened."

Mr. Stedman leaned forward and frowned. "Look, if I were you, Sarah, I would leave out the section about bear poaching in your school project. It can be a nasty, dangerous business and no one really wants to hear about that. Besides, you don't want to have to read about all the terrible things people do to bears. You'll have plenty to say without getting into poaching — that's a whole topic in itself."

He stood up, scraping his chair back behind him. "Now, I believe you two need to get back to school. I have a meeting over that way. Why don't I drive you back?"

We accepted his ride — good thing he offered, we would have been late otherwise. He chatted about school with us and told us to say hi to Cori for him. There was no more mention of bears — or poaching.

"Thank you for meeting with us, Mr. Stedman," I said, as we got out of his Jeep in front of the school.

"Yes," added Mindi, "you've been very helpful."

He nodded. "I hope so," he said. "Those pamphlets I gave you will help. There are links to some websites listed in them in case you need more information."

We thanked him again before he drove off.

"So much for letting me do all the talking," I said with a smirk as we walked towards the school entrance.

Mindi shrugged. “I had to ask.”

“I wish we’d had a chance to ask him more questions. Why didn’t you warn me that he was such a talker? I couldn’t get a word in, then by the time he finally stopped talking long enough for me to ask him a question, it was just about time to leave,” I complained. “What a waste of time! We’re no further ahead than we were this morning.”

Mindi sighed. “We did find out that poaching isn’t a big problem here in Muskoka. That was something.”

“Yeah, I guess so. Why did he have to blab on so much about stuff we didn’t need to know?” I moaned.

“Was that my dad’s car?” asked a shrill voice.

Mindi and I stopped short. Cori was sitting on the stairs at the front of the school with Stacey, staring right at us, her face wearing the scowl she usually reserved for me. She stood up and walked towards us.

“Did you two just get out of my dad’s car?” she asked in disbelief. Mindi opened her mouth and shut it again.

“Yes. He dropped us off after we went to interview him,” I answered, boldly.

Cori’s face reddened. She looked at Mindi. “Why is Sarah’s project so important that you had to go with her and miss having lunch with us?” she asked. “You, me, and Stacey have had lunch together every day at school since grade four.”

“Cori, I ...” Mindi began. “I had to go with her, that’s all. I’ll have lunch with you tomorrow. What’s the big deal?”

Cori looked at her. “There’s something you’re not telling me.”

Mindi made a face. "What are you talking about? We talked to your dad about Sarah's project. If you had brought Sarah a book or two like you said you were going to, we wouldn't have had to go see him ourselves. Look!" She snatched the notebook out of my hands and pulled out the pamphlets Mr. Stedman gave us. "See! Bears. That's all Sarah wanted to know about. For her project. It wouldn't have killed you to help out a little." She turned and stormed into the school leaving me standing there with Cori and Stacey, all of us wearing identical shocked expressions on our faces.

Cori yelled, "Wait, Mindi!" Then, shooting me a look that would have sizzled a piece of bacon, she bolted into the school after Mindi.

Stacey looked at me. "What's going on?"

"I don't know. I'm just trying to do a project," I answered.

BEARS

Black Bears of North America

Full-grown adult black bears weigh between one hundred and six hundred pounds. The colour of their shaggy fur ranges from white to brown and black. Bears are classified as carnivores, but they are really omnivores, meaning they will eat just about anything. They particularly love fresh leaves, nuts, roots, fruits, berries, and tubers.

Bears customarily walk on all four legs. Their hind legs are slightly longer than their front legs. They walk flat-footed. They are able to stand and even walk on their hind legs only. Bears' paws have five non-retractable claws. They are very strong.

Each fall, bears must eat large amounts of food in order to gain sufficient body fat to live off of during their winter hibernation. Bears hibernate in dens. Dens tend to be in caves, under overturned trees, under piles of debris, or in excavated holes.

Black bears usually live in forests, but they can also be found in habitats ranging from swamps to desert scrub. Female bears tend to stay within a small, defined living range throughout their lifetime. Males tend to wander throughout a large area, somewhat less predictably.

Needless to say, Dad, I was having quite an emotional day. First I had to deal with Roy's antics in the gym by the basketball team posting, then I had a disappointing interview with Mr. Stedman, and finally I watched Mindi lose it at Cori. Sure, don't get me wrong, I thought Cori deserved it, but judging by the look she gave me before running off after Mindi to beg forgiveness, I was the one who would be blamed for Mindi's outburst. One more reason for Cori to hate me. Sigh.

As if that wasn't enough, the day continued to go downhill from there. After school, I tried to sneak off on my bike before Mom noticed and enforced your stupid chaperon rule, but I wasn't fast enough, and Roy was told to go with me.

You guessed it, we went to the farmhouse.

CAUGHT?

DATE: FRIDAY, SEPTEMBER 28 (CONTINUED)

LOCATION: THE FARMHOUSE

As soon as we arrived, Mindi and I immediately went about the usual routine of cleaning stalls. Mindi got Roy to fill the horses' water buckets. You should have seen him. He complained the whole time: the buckets were heavy, he slopped water on his pants, and so on. What a wimp.

"You guys do this for fun?" he asked, grunting under the weight of the sloshing water bucket he was carrying.

"It'll build up the muscles in your weak little arms," I retorted.

He set down the bucket and made a big show of flexing his tiny biceps. "Who's got weak arms?" he asked, wiggling his eyebrows at Mindi.

She giggled. I was getting worried about her. She was really getting taken in by this joker. I planned to have a little chat with her later to set her straight.

When we were done our chores, Mindi and I saddled up Ginger and Candy. We were going to ride down the trail again. Roy continued to be a pain.

"So what am I supposed to do while you two are riding the horses?" he asked. "Last time you took forever."

"You could come with us," offered Mindi. "Thunder would love some exercise, wouldn't you, old boy?"

At the mention of his name, Thunder whinnied and tossed his head up and down as if saying "yes." We all laughed.

"No thanks," said Roy, eyeing Thunder, who kicked the side of his stall in agitation. "You told me before that he wasn't a good horse for a beginner. Believe me, I'm a beginner."

"Well, I guess that's that," I said with a shrug.

"So I'm just supposed to sit here?" asked Roy with a scowl.

"Well, if you're bored ..." started Mindi. "Nah, you won't want to."

"What? What can I do?"

"You see these?" She pulled some leather bridles down from their hooks in the tack room. "These really need to be cleaned, and I know Colin hasn't had time to do it. He'd really appreciate it."

"You want me to sit here and clean leather straps?" He didn't look thrilled. I had to laugh at the thought of Roy doing manual labour — something he generally avoided like the plague.

"Only if you want to," assured Mindi. She was too nice. Didn't she know that Roy would rather sit around doing nothing but thinking about himself than do work?

"Look," I said. I was starting to get impatient with Lazy-Boy. "Here are your choices: a) ride Thunder and come with us; b) make yourself useful and clean the bridles while you wait; or c) sit here and do nothing but be a waste of skin. What's it going to be?"

Roy looked at Mindi and sighed. "All right, how do I clean these stupid straps?"

Mindi and I took the same route as we did the last time we rode the horses down the trail, wordlessly tying the horses up at the same trees. This wasn't preplanned. It just happened. It was like our minds were synchronized. We skirted around the field through the forest towards the forbidden barn. The coast was clear so we dashed out to our makeshift doorway.

"Follow me, partner," I said, and pulled away the loose boards.

Mindi's eyebrows rose when she saw the larger opening I had created. It was now a lot easier for us to get inside the barn than it was for me to get out the other day. She squeezed in behind me and carefully pulled the boards back into place as best as she could to cover up the evidence of our entry.

We were immediately immersed in the musty odour of bears. I stood for a moment allowing my eyes to adjust to the relative dimness after the bright daylight. I was determined to get a much better look around than I did during my previous visit. I led the way and we began to shuffle along behind the row of cages, our backs against the rough barn wall. Mindi was wide-eyed as she took it all in.

As we made our way behind the cages, the bear in front of us swung his massive head in our direction, eyeing us curiously. Mindi froze and stared back at him. I knew how she felt. It was easy to forget they were in cages when you were this close.

"Keep moving, Mindi," I instructed, giving her a gentle pull.

Finally, we turned the corner, shuffled past the last cage, and emerged into the middle corridor of the barn. We stood there and gazed down at the long rows of cages on either side of us.

"I can't believe it," whispered Mindi. "I mean, I *believed* you when you told me, but this is incredible. These poor bears."

"I know." I started to walk down the middle of the corridor. It was a whole lot easier to do this when it wasn't so dark and you had someone beside you. Strength in numbers, I guess. "Walk quietly," I instructed, "last time I was here, the bears went ape when I made noise."

Mindi giggled nervously, making me giggle. So far the bears weren't paying a whole lot of attention to us. As we walked I looked into each of the cages to look for any signs that the bears were being tapped for bile. To be honest, I wasn't exactly sure of what I was looking for — tubes and vials, I supposed. We travelled all the way to the other end of the corridor and were standing in front of the door that led to the small front room when we heard them come in.

We froze — like deer caught in headlights. I wanted to run but had no idea where to run to.

"I told you that I require appointments. I can't have you and Mr. Cheng just showing up here whenever you feel like it," said Mr. Braemarie's irritated voice from the front room.

"We like to keep tabs on our investments and make sure they are being well taken care of," explained another voice. "And about that other matter, we don't understand why it's a problem. We were under the impression that we could easily make the necessary arrangements for shipment."

"Mr. Gorely, like I already explained, I'm running a small operation here. To supply the number of bear galls and paws that you're asking for and to have them prepared for delivery by next Saturday is just impossible for me."

Mindi and I looked at each other with wide eyes.

"There should be no problem, Mr. Braemarie. I'm getting the impression that you're stalling on making good with your delivery. I have buyers waiting and they're getting impatient," said Gorely.

Mr. Braemarie continued, "All I'm suggesting is that you take about half of your shipment next week. The other half will only take me another two to four weeks to pull together. No problem. If you give me the names of your buyers, I can deliver the goods directly myself."

"No," said Gorely in clipped tones. "Our buyers work only through us, and like I said, they are getting extremely impatient for these bear parts. I will not wait any longer; either you deliver the full order next Saturday or we don't have a deal."

We heard a shuffling sound and a thud, and the door in front of us trembled as if with an impact. We jumped back and clutched each other's hands.

"I'm telling you now," said Gorely in his steely voice, "and believe me when I say this: I am not a patient man. And as you can see, Mr. Cheng is also not a patient man. We're used to having things our way, and anyone who denies us is soon ... out of the picture, so to speak. You do understand what I'm saying, don't you?"

"I got it," gasped Mr. Braemarie. "Now, tell Mr. Cheng to let me go. There's no need to get rough." We heard more shuffling.

"Consider this a friendly warning, Mr. Braemarie."

Mr. Braemarie cleared his throat. "I don't like threats, Mr. Gorely, but I will try to find some way to come up with the full order. You want five live bears, correct?"

"Correct."

"You see, that just complicates the delivery arrangements somewhat ..." More shuffling noises. "... but I'll figure it out," Mr. Braemarie croaked.

"I knew you'd be able to make things work for us, Mr. Braemarie," crooned Gorely. I could almost hear an evil smile as he spoke. "We'll expect everything to be ready next Saturday, at dawn. We'll need an early start. It's been a pleasure doing business with you."

We listened as the men left. My body sagged with relief and Mindi slumped to the floor. The sound of Mr. Braemarie's voice made us freeze in horror once again. We had thought he left with the other men.

"Pleasure doing business, my ..." he mumbled from the front room.

Mr. Braemarie's chair squeaked. A drawer was opened, then shut. We heard the quiet beeps of a cell phone being turned on.

"Colin here," he said curtly, after a moment. "Yeah. Gorely and Cheng were here. Just showed up, no call, no nothing. I didn't even have time to get my gun. This is getting out of hand, they got a bit rough. And listen to this, they want more than we were prepared for ... Uh-huh. Plus five live ones ... No, I can probably arrange it, but ... No, they wouldn't give me any of the buyers' names ..." A longer pause followed. "Okay. That'll work. Yes, next Saturday at dawn .... Right ... That'll do."

I stole a glance at Mindi; her eyes were like saucers. Mr. Braemarie muttered to himself and his chair squeaked again.

"It's dinner time!" he yelled, and footsteps swiftly approached the door that was hiding us from him.

What happened next outlines the real beginning of Roy's involvement with the bears. Mindi and I never planned to tell him that we were working together to clear Mr. Braemarie's name, but you know Roy, he tends to do the unexpected. The way I see it, none of us was really to blame. Let's face it, Dad, if you hadn't created that new rule about me not biking alone, then Roy would never have been near that farmhouse in the first place. He never would have gone there on his own. So I guess it was kind of your fault that Roy got involved.

It's another way of looking at it.

Caught!

Date: Friday, September 28 (continued)

Location: Barn and Stable

So there we were, inside the forbidden barn, frozen right behind the door that Mr. Braemarie was about to walk through. Scared to death. Unable to move. We'd be caught for sure. That realization was like a starting gun in my head.

Blindly, I shoved Mindi into the dark corner on our right, behind the first cage. She quickly caught on. Mr. Braemarie banged into the room just as we hunkered down into the shadows, making ourselves as small as possible. He didn't look our way as he headed straight for the supply cage. He pulled the wheelbarrow upright, loaded it up with buckets full of slop from the smelly pig slop barrels, and grabbed a tub of stinky chicken and fish from the fridge. Then he pushed the wheelbarrow, laden with buckets, out into the corridor. My heart was jumping around in my chest as if on a trampoline. I clutched Mindi's shoulder tightly. I was actually thankful for the dim natural lighting, thankful for the shadowy corners.

"Hey old guys," Mr. Braemarie crooned, "are you hungry?"

To our horror, the bear in the cage we hid behind lumbered over towards our corner, sniffing the air. Mr. Braemarie noticed and turned back, a playful smile on his lips.

"What are you sniffing at? You know I can't keep the mice out of here," he chuckled. "You're just going to have to get used to them."

I held my breath. Mindi and I tried to be absolute statues. I was thankful for my black jeans and dark shirt. Without moving my head, I shifted my glance to Mindi. Her eyes were squeezed shut and her hands were clenched under her chin as if in prayer. It reminded me of the old game I used to play with Roy when I was a little kid. You know the one: No one could see you if you couldn't see them. All you had to do to hide was shut your eyes.

The bear gave the air one last sniff then jerked its head away with a grunt and lumbered over to the front of his cage.

"Did you scare those big bad mice away?" laughed Mr. Braemarie. To my alarm, he actually reached into the cage and rubbed the bear's head. "I've got you some food."

It was a miracle. He didn't see us! I let my breath out slowly and touched Mindi gently on her arm. Her eyes flew open and I tried to give her a reassuring smile. I'm not so sure how it turned out though.

We watched as Mr. Braemarie slowly made his way down the corridor between the cages, tossing food slops from the buckets into the cages. The bears were ecstatic, diving onto the food with grunts of pleasure. They ate like pigs, which is why, I guess, they liked that pig slop. Kind of reminded me of Roy at the dinner table.

Mr. Braemarie then unwound the hose and used it to pour fresh water into the pails that hung in each cage. If I weren't so scared, I would have found it very interesting to watch. Heck, even scared, it was interesting. It was like being at a zoo during feeding time. Except it wasn't a zoo, I realized with a pang that took the pleasure out of it. If only those poor bears knew what was in store for them. At least they were being treated well before being brutally slaughtered and mercilessly sold for profit.

Finally, chores done, Mr. Braemarie stood at the door and surveyed his bear farm — I was positive that's what it was, even though I still hadn't seen any tubes or complicated machinery. Mindi and I had another terror-filled moment as he did this, certain that this time we would be seen. His eyes swept dangerously close to our hiding spot, but it was pretty dark in our corner. We remained still while he left the cage-room and stayed frozen until we heard the outer door of the barn slam shut and the padlock click into place. A good five minutes of silence later, we finally dared to speak.

"Is he really gone?" whispered Mindi, wide-eyed.

"I think so," I whispered back.

"*Oh my gosh*! I thought for sure he'd see us!" bawled Mindi, grabbing my arm. "I've never been so scared in my life."

"Me neither. I thought we were goners," I agreed.

We struggled to our feet within the tight quarters. Quickly, we shuffled down the narrow corridor towards our small hidden doorway. We were both anxious to get out of that barn. Mindi kicked out the loose boards and we crawled to freedom. I was so close behind her I could have kissed her shoe. Instead, once I crawled out and was on the grass, I kissed the ground.

"I love you, grass!" I said, kissing the ground loudly. "We're free!" Laughing, I rolled onto my back to look up at Mindi.

Roy's angry face stared down at me.

"Uh-oh," I murmured, then jumped to my feet.

Mindi was standing behind him, staring down at the ground sheepishly. The best defence is a good offence, I always say.

"What are you doing here?" I demanded angrily.

"What are *you* doing here?" he shot back. His voice rose to an unflattering shriek. "Sarah, you promised me you would stay away from this barn. You told me you were just coming here to visit with Mindi and to ride horses, and I believed you! Now I find you sneaking out of Mr. Braemarie's barn. The one you told me that he warned you to stay away from." He began pacing in front of us. "I should have known I couldn't trust you — that you couldn't keep your nose out of other people's business. Our deal's off, I'm not coming here with you anymore."

"No, Roy, let me explain. I can explain everything," I pleaded, grabbing his arm.

"Sarah," interrupted Mindi as she hurriedly replaced the barn boards to conceal the small doorway. "We should probably get away from here. Just in case Colin comes back."

"Right," I agreed. "Roy, let's talk about this somewhere else."

Roy looked from Mindi to me, then back to Mindi again. Slowly he nodded. "Okay. Let's go. This had better be good."

We made our way back to the tethered horses. Mindi gave me a leg up onto Ginger. Roy helped Mindi onto Candy. Then he walked alongside us as we plodded back to the stable.

I couldn't stay quiet anymore. "So what exactly were you doing at the barn anyway, Roy? Planning to do a little spying on your own? Couldn't resist seeing for yourself what was going on in the mysterious barn?"

Roy looked up at me coldly. "You were taking forever. I finished cleaning those leather straps ages ago and I got sick of sitting there waiting by myself. So I walked down the trail thinking I'd catch you guys on your way back. Instead, I found your horses tied up to a tree. I knew right away what you were up to."

"It's not what you think."

"Uh-huh."

Back at the stable, we quickly removed saddles, exchanged bridles for halters, and led the horses out to the field. Then Mindi pulled the big doors shut and pulled out some stools for us to sit on. She looked miserable.

Roy perched himself on a stool, folded his arms in front of him, and looked at us expectantly.

"Well?"

I did most of the talking. I explained how Mindi came to be suspicious about Mr. Braemarie and the contents of the barn and how we wanted to clear his name. Then I told him exactly what we just heard Mr. Braemarie and the men talking about. I'll give him some credit, he at least let me finish before pronouncing judgement.

"So this confirms it," he concluded.

"Confirms what?" I asked.

"It's time for you two to step out and let the police deal with this. It's become way too dangerous," he stood up. "I'll go with you to talk to Dad, if that helps."

I stared at him as if he were crazy. "I'm not going to Dad with this!"

"Yes, you are."

"Roy! He already knows. Remember the file? The one you wouldn't let me read? Nothing I could tell him will change anything. I'd only get into trouble for being here. I'd be grounded forever — but oh, you'd like that, wouldn't you?" I scowled.

"What file?" asked Mindi, puzzled.

I bit my lip. Yikes! I had never told her about the file. I explained sheepishly, "I looked in my dad's briefcase one day and saw a file with Mr. Braemarie's name on it. I was about to look inside it but Roy caught me and locked the briefcase before I had a chance."

"So all this time you knew there was something bad going on with Colin? Why didn't you say something?" She looked hurt.

"Mindi, it could have been anything — or nothing — and I didn't think it was my place to say. I had no idea then that it had something to do with poaching bears," I explained.

She still looked hurt. "I thought we were partners."

"We are!"

"Partners tell each other everything," she said, pouting.

"I will from now on," I promised in earnest. "No more secrets, I swear."

"Look, this is very nice and all," interrupted Roy, "but what are we going to do? If what you say is true —"

"It is! Every word," I protested.

"— then we need to let Dad know about next Saturday," he finished.

"He's right," sighed Mindi. "The police need to know; we need to tell them."

"I still can't believe there's a bunch of bears caged up in that barn," said Roy, shaking his head.

"Why don't you go and look for yourself if you don't believe us," I challenged him.

Roy looked thoughtful. "Maybe I should, so that when we go to Dad I can be sure you don't forget to tell him something crucial."

I couldn't believe my ears. What a hypocrite!

"Oh, so it's okay for you to go in the barn, but when we do, it's a felony," I said.

He shrugged. "If I'm going to Dad with this, I want to know what I'm talking about."

I rolled my eyes. It's always all about Roy with him.

"We can't go back in there now," said Mindi. "It's getting late, and we have to get the horses back to the stable. Come back tomorrow morning. Mom and Colin are planning to go into town and I was going to hang out here with the horses."

"Tomorrow morning, then." Roy nodded grimly. I sighed. He could be a little overdramatic.

Dad, I know you might want to blame me for Roy going into that barn, but honestly, I didn't really think he would. In fact, I would have made a million-dollar bet that he wouldn't go near that barn, otherwise, I would never have said that. As you read on, remember, you're the one who made up the chaperon rule.

Besides, I think the real reason he wanted to go into the barn was plain old curiosity. I'm the one that always gets busted for this, but Roy's got his share too. Plus, he wouldn't want Mindi to think he was scared. You should have seen the goo-goo eyes he was making at her that day; it was sickening.

I ended up having to drag Romeo away from the farm so that we wouldn't get shot for being late for dinner. It was rather disgusting. The worst part was that Mindi was just as bad as he was! I was starting to feel like a fifth wheel.

I really needed to talk some sense into that girl.

And as if making eyes at my friend wasn't bad enough, Dad, let me recount for you a little conversation I had with Roy tonight. It went something like this:

"Boy, you sure write a lot of crap!" Roy said, slamming down the notebook containing the latest pages of my report.

"So you keep telling me," I said, "but where are you when I'm cooped up in my room slugging it all out? I write what happened and that's it. Besides, what are you complaining about? I'm making sure that you look totally innocent in all this. Don't worry, Daddy still thinks you're his perfect son."

"Yeah, bribing you to buy my silence about your visits to the farmhouse, that looks really innocent," he complained.

"It's true though, isn't it?" I reminded him.

He frowned. "Only at first. Once I decided to go into that barn with you, I was in it as much as you. There was nothing to bribe you about. And this stuff about Mindi and I ... you don't have to include that in your report."

I shrugged. "Dad said to include everything. I said that's what I'd do."

Roy threw up his hands in exasperation and fell back in his chair. "Okay, well, I have another complaint."

I just rolled my eyes. "I'm sure you do."

"That whole section you wrote about making the basketball team, what does that have to do with Mr. Braemarie's barn?"

"Nothing."

"Why did you include it then?"

"I wanted Mom and Dad to know how you treat me at school. That was really embarrassing, you know, especially with everyone there, watching all of it. You're lucky I did make the team, it could have been really humiliating."

Roy waved me off. "I told you, I already *knew* you made the team. I checked the list before you even got there. Do you really think I'd do all that if there was a chance you didn't make it? I'm not that cold-hearted. I wouldn't deliberately embarrass you — *that* much."

"Oh, well, isn't that the nicest thing you've ever said to me."

"Besides," he continued, "how would that have made me look to my fan club? I wouldn't want the girls to think I was mean to my little sister. Where would that get me with any of them?"

"Ugh! You're such a pig," I said, punching his leg. "I should have known you had you in mind the whole time."

He laughed. "I'm just joking, relax. But about this report, you can't give it to Dad the way it is."

"Really? Go on," I said, while clenching my teeth.

"Like I've already said. You're deliberately trying to make me look like an idiot. You make fun of Mindi and me, and you make me sound like I'm a lazy lump. I'm getting tired of this abuse."

"Truth hurts, eh?" I shook my head as if I felt sympathy. "I suppose you could do a better job?"

"That's goes without saying."

That was it. I was sick of his constant whining and complaining. I threw the notebook at him. "Good. Be my guest. Take over."

"Now wait a minute, Dad said you're supposed to do it." He stooped over and gathered up the fallen book.

"Do you think I care at this point? I'm tired of it. So if you think you're capable of sitting still for longer than ten minutes, go ahead."

"I'm capable."

"I'll believe it when I see it."

"You'll see it."

"Uh-huh."

And that's how it went, Dad. That's why the next few pages are written by His Majesty, the one and only Roy.

The Best,
Most Complete,
Most Honest
Part of this Report
by Roy

Hey Dad, I'm writing this part of the report myself because I thought you deserved to know the truth, for once, of what happened when Sarah (against my wishes!) talked me into going into the forbidden barn with her and Mindi. Believe me, I tried to tell her that we should just go straight to you, but she seemed to think it was important to show me what was in the barn first. You know how she gets when her mind's made up. If I didn't go along with her, she would have just gone in alone, and who knows what kind of trouble she would have gotten into without me there keeping an eye on her.

Also, I'm getting really tired of all the written abuse I've been taking in this report. You know that I'm not the schmuck that Sarah keeps making me out to be, don't you? I don't care what she says, I don't constantly embarrass her in front of other people — she does that to herself — and I don't always act like a goof. In fact, I'm very responsible, and I wanted you to read that for once. You know, the truth.

So here's the real story of the day Sarah, Mindi, and I went into the forbidden barn at Mr. Braemarie's farmhouse.

Remember, she made me do it. And remember, I told her to go to you!

Saturday, September 29

Right after breakfast, Sarah and I got ready to take off for Mr. Braemarie's farm. Just before we left, Mom pulled me aside.

"Roy," she said, "you've been so terrific about taking care of your little sister all this past week. I don't know what I would have done without you."

"It's been no problem, Mom," I said, smiling in my usual charming way. "Anything to help."

"You don't have to stick with Sarah today. You have a break, do what you want to do for a change. I'll keep Sarah here with me."

"Mom," whined Sarah from the doorway, "we're going to go on a bike ride, right, Roy?"

"Mom, it's okay. I don't mind," I said with a sigh.

She gave me a big hug. "You're the best son a mother could have."

She always says stuff like that.

Soon, Sarah and I were cycling down the road towards the farmhouse. I, as usual, was able to travel at a high velocity — at least Mach 2. Since I know that Sarah hates to be left behind, I patiently kept letting her catch up to me. Unlike what she thinks, I am a thoughtful guy. She was pretty red-faced and out of breath trying to keep up with me. She really needs to work out a little more.

"Anxious to get there and see your new girlfriend, Roy?" she yelled at me between breaths. That's what I get for being nice and letting her catch up. I ignored her and pedalled a teeny bit harder so that she fell behind and stayed there.

I was leaning my bike against a tree by the driveway just as Mindi stepped out onto the front porch of Mr. Braemarie's house. She gave me a huge smile and waved as Sarah just about fell off her bike behind me.

"Nobody's home," Mindi called out. "Mom and Colin went into town as planned. They'll probably be back by lunch."

"That's perfect!" said Sarah. "We won't have to worry about getting caught — again." At that she shot me a look. I grinned back.

We headed straight for the barn. It was windy and cool that day. Mindi pulled her nylon jacket together at the front and shivered. "You know, I still can't believe Colin would do something to hurt bears," she said.

I could see that she was upset so I tried to make her feel better. "Maybe there's some other explanation," I suggested. "Maybe you guys are missing something."

"We're not missing anything," retorted Sarah, cruelly.

Mindi looked even sadder at that. Sarah can be very insensitive. She didn't even notice that she hurt Mindi's feelings.

We walked down the side of the barn to the secret opening that I'd caught the girls coming out of the day before. Mindi bent down and pulled away the loose boards. She motioned for me to enter, but before I could, Sarah pushed in front of me and crawled through herself. Like a gentleman, I stepped aside so Mindi could go next. I followed, pulling the boards back in place behind me, just in case someone arrived home early and took a walk along the side of his barn.

By the time Mindi and I squeezed out from between the cages and the back wall, Sarah had already walked to the other end of the barn, looking for who knows what.

The barn was amazing! Very cool! There were bears everywhere, well, in their cages — you know what I mean.

"Oh, wow! I don't believe this," I whispered to Mindi.

"Isn't it awesome?" she asked.

I nodded. We slowly walked down the long passage between the two rows of cages, looking inside each of them as we passed. It was like our own personal zoo. One of the bears was staring at me so I stopped and stared back.

"Here bear," I called to him, snapping my fingers through the bars.

"They aren't pets, Roy. You don't call them like they're dogs or something," said Sarah from the other side of the barn.

The bear huffed back at me and we continued to glare at each other. I've never been that close to a bear before. What was he thinking? Did he wonder how I'd taste with ketchup?

"So you two actually heard Mr. Braemarie talking to people about buying parts from these bears?" I asked Mindi, keeping my eye glued to the staring bear.

"Yeah, and it sounded like some of the bears are going to be sold alive, too," she answered.

I frowned. "I just don't know. Are you sure that's what he meant? Maybe you thought they were talking about these bears but they were really talking about something else," I suggested.

"Roy!" yelled Sarah. "Look around you! What else would they have been talking about?"

"I'm just saying we have to think this through. You know, think about all possibilities and not jump to any conclusions," I said, very reasonably and logically.

Sarah threw a little hissy fit. If I wasn't so embarrassed for her, I'd have laughed. "Roy, come here if you're so smart," she ordered, pushing open a door at the far end of the barn. I tore my eyes away from the staring contest I was having with the bear and followed Sarah into a small dark room at the front of the barn. Inside the room, there was a desk and a couple of chairs. A ladder leaned against the wall to the right, leading up to an even darker loft. Sarah pulled open the lower left-hand drawer of the desk and pointed.

"So what's that there for?" she demanded.

I took a look.

"Whoa, cool!" I gave a low whistle when I saw the gun inside. I stepped forward to pick it up. Sarah slapped my hand away. Hard.

"Are you crazy? Don't touch it!" she shrieked, then slammed the drawer shut.

"I can touch it, I fire Dad's gun all the time. I know what I'm doing," I said, pushing her aside.

"Only when you're at the range and he's supervising," she argued. "Besides, haven't you ever heard of fingerprints? Do you really want to leave yours all over the gun?"

"You've already left yours all over the drawer!" I yelled back.

She stared at me, then yanked down the bottom of her T-shirt and frantically wiped off the drawer's handle with it. I shook my head. Good thing I was there to do the thinking.

"Roy, if we're right about Colin and the men he's been dealing with, these bears only have until next Saturday to live," Mindi said. "And I think we might be. These men mean business. They're scary. Why else would Colin keep a gun?" Her lower lip trembled as she pointed back to the desk.

She was really upset and she was looking at me for help. I knew just what we had to do.

"We have to tell my dad right away," I said. "He's a police detective, he'll be able to deal with this properly. It's our only option."

Sarah stopped wiping the drawer with her T-shirt and frowned. "You're right, Roy."

"Pardon me, Sarah, I didn't quite catch that." I leaned one ear towards her as if to help myself hear better.

She scowled at me. "Grow up!" she barked, then rudely turned her back on me and spoke to Mindi.

"Since I'm going to get into trouble anyway for being in this barn against orders," she said, "then while I'm here I might as well look around for more evidence to tell my dad about — you know, make it really worthwhile."

"Does she think she's the only one in trouble for being in here? What more evidence does she think we need anyway?" I asked Mindi as we followed Sarah back to the larger room where the bears were. She shrugged, obviously as confused as I was about Sarah's self-centred thinking.

Mindi and I made our way towards the back of the barn as Sarah ran around and into dark corners looking for who knows what. The bears seemed well cared for. I mean, they stunk and they didn't look the cleanest, but they all had food and water in their cages. Heck, they were lively enough. A couple of them came right up to the front of their cages to sniff at us as we passed.

Mindi sighed. "They're such beautiful animals. I can't believe people would want to kill them for their gallbladders and their paws and stuff." She shuddered.

I nodded sympathetically, while looking around for Sarah.

Then I heard her yelling, "Come here, you guys!"

This unexpected noise startled the bears and the whole barn filled with grunts and the sound of claws scraping on bars. Apparently, Sarah's voice has a soothing effect on animals.

"You gotta see this. I'm in the far corner." Her voice came from behind one of the cages, the one to the left of the door leading to the front room. We hurried over.

Suddenly, Sarah's head appeared as if from out of nowhere. Her eyes were wide with excitement.

"I found a hidden room," she said excitedly. "Come on!"

Sarah stood inside a room the size of a large walk-in closet. A dingy, bare bulb was the only light, a dirty string hanging from its chain. Taking up most of the space was a large rectangular deep freezer, like the one we have at home. The wall across from the freezer was lined with several shelves that were piled high with dusty tools, bottles of liquid, things that might have been medical instruments, and …

"Wow!" I exclaimed as I forgot all about fingerprints and picked up what looked like an air rifle, turning it over in my hands. "This looks like a tranquilizer gun," I told the girls. "I've seen them on the Discovery Channel. See this? That's where you put the dart, you put in one at a time, right here."

"Put it down, Roy! Don't swing that thing our way," screeched Sarah, holding up a hand as if to ward off an attack. I pretended to shoot her. It didn't even have a dart loaded in it and she just about fainted in fright.

Mindi stood wide-eyed. "What's in the freezer?" she asked, her voice shaky.

"I don't know, but there's one way to find out," I said, putting the tranquilizer gun back on the shelf.

Sarah pushed up the freezer's lid. An interior light came on, making Sarah and Mindi's faces glow as they looked inside.

"It's just a bunch of brown packages like you get from the butcher." Mindi sighed with relief.

"Yeah?" I asked, looking over their shoulders. "What's in them? Pot roasts?"

The girls looked at each other, then Sarah scooped up one of the packages and bounced it in her hand a little as if testing its weight. She carefully picked at the end of the brittle tape holding the paper closed then peeled it back, unwrapping the package. Underneath, clear cellophane caught the light of the bare bulb. Sarah frowned and turned it this way and that.

"What is it?" asked Mindi, leaning in closer. We examined it with growing horror.

"It looks like …" I began, frowning.

"… a bear's paw!" finished Sarah, dropping it back into the freezer. "Ugh!" She frantically wiped her hands on her pant legs.

Mindi's face went white. "Do you think all these packages are … paws?"

"Some might be gallbladders," Sarah said, dully.

Mindi turned away holding her hands to her mouth. "I think I'm going to be sick," she said weakly.

"Me, too!" gasped Sarah, clutching her stomach.

"You two need to get out of here," I said. "I'll wrap that thing back up and put it away."

But the girls were falling apart. It was one thing to read about poachers and what they did to bears but to actually hold a severed bear part in your own hands … they were pretty shaken up. I'd have to take charge.

I put an arm around both girls' shoulders and gently led them out of the tiny room.

"The paw …" started Sarah weakly.

"Don't worry," I assured her. "I'll take care of it."

With the girls holding onto my strong arms, I led them to the back of the barn and in behind the cages towards our little doorway, coaxing them as they shuffled along as if in shock by what they had seen. Once I made sure they were safely outside, I hurried back to the hidden room to cover our tracks.

It was easier to think without two hysterical girls on either side of me. I carefully wrapped the paw back up in the brown paper and taped it into place. It didn't look as neatly packaged as before and the tape wasn't very sticky anymore, but it held. I stood back to admire my work. There sure were a lot of packages in that freezer. If they were all bear parts, then a lot of bears must have been killed to get them. I swallowed hard. Sarah wanted more evidence and I guess she found it. I closed the lid on the freezer, pulled the string to turn off the overhead bulb, and left the tiny room, pulling the door shut behind me. Mr. Braemarie would never know anyone was in there.

As I walked back down the long passage between the cages, I was aware of the eyes sombrely watching my progress. I couldn't shake the feeling that the bears somehow knew what I had seen in that room. I couldn't look at them now without thinking of that hard, frozen paw; I wondered if it came from a friend of theirs. What was in store for these bears?

The two girls were sitting on the grass, leaning against the outer wall, when I crawled out of the barn. They watched glumly as I replaced the boards and returned everything to normal.

"Thank you, Roy," said Mindi. "We should have stayed and helped."

"Don't worry," I said. "You were too upset. I didn't mind." She smiled at me gratefully.

"What would we have done without you?" she asked. I sat down beside her.

"Are you okay?" I put my hand gently on her arm. She nodded, her eyes moist.

"Yeah, and I'm okay too, Roy. Thanks for asking," butted in Sarah from the other side of Mindi.

"What are we going to do?" Mindi cried. "We can't just stand around and watch that freezer fill up with more paws and ... other things." She shuddered. "We have to stop it!"

Sarah nodded. "Roy, what do you think we should do? We have to stop Mr. Braemarie and those men from hurting any more bears."

I knew exactly what needed to be done.

"We have to tell Dad about this right now," I said. "That's the only solution."

"Roy's right," agreed Mindi. "This is too big to keep quiet anymore. There are absolutely no doubts left about what Colin's doing with those bears." She blinked back tears. "This is really going to upset my mom. I'm sure she doesn't know anything about this. She's belongs to the Wildlife Foundation — there's no way she'd knowingly have anything to do with someone who would poach bears, or any other animal."

We sat a bit longer. I didn't know what to say. Mindi was upset, so I put my arm around her to comfort her. Finally, Sarah stood up.

"Let's get this over with. Say goodbye to me 'cause as soon as we tell Dad about being in this barn I'll be grounded for the rest of my life. It'll be all my fault, just wait and see." She started walking towards the house. "It's been nice knowing ya."

We were quiet on the bike ride home. I doubled Mindi and still beat Sarah there. They followed me to Dad's study. He was working at his desk; it was piled high with files and papers. I knocked before walking in, the girls stood behind me. Dad scowled at the disturbance.

"Hi, Dad," I said.

"Hi, kids," he replied, not looking up from the papers on his desk.

"You look a little busy," Sarah noted, needlessly.

"You bet I am."

He set down his pen and swivelled around in his chair to face us. "I'm telling you," he began, wagging a finger in our direction. The wagging finger was never a good sign. "I spend more time dealing with runaway kids, kids on drugs, and kids doing all-nighters worrying their parents to death. I spent all last night dealing with juvenile delinquents and now I'm swamped in the paperwork. Just think how much time I'd have to go after the real criminals of this world if kids would just listen to their parents!"

"Maybe we caught you at a bad time," said Sarah, biting her lip and backing away.

Dad put his finger down. "It's very frustrating," he said, then sighed. "At least I don't have to deal with this kind of thing in my own home." He looked right at Sarah and said, "At least I know my own children follow the rules and don't go running off to places where they shouldn't, right?" He swivelled back around to face his desk and muttered, "If I had to deal with one more case of youth delinquency right now, I think I'd explode." He turned back to us and smiled grimly. "So what's up, kids?"

"Uh ..." stammered Sarah. Her face was white. "Uh ..."

Once again I had to step in and save the day for Sarah. "Nothing, Dad," I said. "We just thought we'd say hi, you know, let you know we're back from biking." I nudged Mindi forward. "Have you met Mindi yet, Dad?" I threw Sarah a look, to get her to introduce her friend. She wasn't getting it. She was still stuttering. I sighed and introduced Mindi to Dad for her.

Then, I got the girls out of there. We escaped to the rec room. Good plans need to have good timing, and this was not the best time for telling Dad about Mr. Braemarie's barn.

So much for Plan A.

Can you believe that load of garbage? Give me a break! There's no way Roy will be writing any more of this report, not that he'd want to anyway. The only reason I'm including his section, Dad, is so you can see what I have to put up with every day — Roy's full-blown, hugely over-estimated opinion of himself. I think he actually believes everything he wrote!

Let me set the record straight ...

First of all, Mom doesn't always tell Roy he's the best son a mother could have. That's just gross! Next, I do not need to work out more. I only stay behind him when we're biking so I don't have to listen to him bragging all the time about how fast he thinks he's going. Mach 2! Whatever! And it wasn't me pushing my way into the barn first. I have more manners than that. In fact, Roy was in the barn and down the corridor looking at the bears before Mindi and I even crawled through the opening.

While he did tell the truth about me being the one to find the freezer room, I wasn't all freaked out by it like he said. Mindi and I were definitely not hysterical. In fact, I was the one who wrapped the paw back up and we left the room and the barn together. Unbelievable! He led us out while we were holding onto his strong arms. I think I'm going to puke!

To think that he has the nerve to talk about me *not getting the facts right. The main reason he wanted to write a part of this report was to make himself look like a hero. Yeah right, some hero. Just remember, Dad, that Roy makes Roy sound good while making me sound bad. It was a little payback for how I've been portraying him, even though I'm just telling the truth. It's so Roy.*

So basically, what he did get right was that the three of us went into the barn together and I found the room with the tranquilizer gun and the freezer full of bear parts. More evidence against Mr. Braemarie. He also got the scene with you pretty much right although I don't remember stuttering!

Do you understand now why we didn't tell you what we knew about the barn that day? You have to believe me, Dad, we were planning to. But we caught you at such a bad time and we really didn't want to make you angrier and more frustrated than you already were. After what you said about us not being disobedient like those other kids you deal with all the time, I just couldn't tell you that for weeks I'd been going to the Braemarie farmhouse against your direct orders. I don't know if you realize it, but you're a little scary when you're mad.

So we didn't tell you what we found in the barn, but this is what we did do …

What To Do?

Date: Saturday, September 29 (continued)

Location: Home

"We can just go to another police officer," suggested Roy. "It doesn't have to be Dad."

"Dad will still find out that it was us that made the report," I pointed out. "We'd get into just as much trouble as if we'd gone to him ourselves."

"True."

"But we have to let the police know somehow," protested Mindi. "They only have till next Saturday to stop Colin from killing the bears."

"Maybe *you* could talk to our dad, Mindi," suggested Roy.

"No way," I protested. "He'd link that to me in an instant. I'd end up getting into trouble and you'd be off the hook, Roy."

"Well, what better ideas do you have?" he asked, crossing his arms.

I frowned. I needed time to think.

"What about Cori's dad? Why don't we go to him?" asked Roy.

"Mr. Gabby?" I asked incredulously. "He'd be no help; he'd probably just talk us out of it. He doesn't even think poaching's a problem here in Muskoka. He'd never believe us."

"We could still call the Ministry of Natural Resources office," argued Roy.

"They're closed on Saturdays," I retorted. "That's why Mindi and I had to make the appointment with Mr. Stedman on a Friday."

Then Mindi had a brainstorm. "Why don't we make an anonymous tip? You know, like they do with Crime Stoppers. Can we do that?" she asked.

"Hey, that could work," said Roy.

I whacked my forehead. "Why didn't I think of that?" I moaned. "I just read about how Ontario has an anti-poaching campaign through Crime Stoppers when I was doing my research. That's perfect! You're the best, Mindi!"

So that's what we did. We just looked up the number in the phone book. It was a lot easier to find than Mr. Stedman's number. Roy did all the talking. He tried to disguise his voice by making it sound really low. If it wasn't so serious, I would have found it funny. Afterwards, there was a heavy feeling of finality. We couldn't take it back; we'd started things in motion that couldn't be reversed.

"Well, I guess that's it," Mindi said as we plunked ourselves down in the rec room. "Colin's going to be arrested and put in jail. My mom's going to be devastated. And I won't be going to his farm anymore to ride his horses. Everything's ruined."

Roy sighed. "Maybe he won't get arrested, Mindi. Maybe he'll just be fined or something. The bottom line is that what he's doing is illegal, and like my dad says, 'all choices have consequences.'"

"Dad says that?" I asked, puzzled.

"Yes, he does, Sarah. Maybe you should listen to him once in a while," Roy suggested. I made a face at him.

"I guess we'll just have to wait and see what happens." Mindi shrugged. "No matter what, I can't see my mom wanting to have any more to do with him after she finds all this out." She shook her head. "And I feel the same way. I don't know how I'll be able to look him in the eye again. What he's doing to these bears is terrible and has to be stopped, no matter what." A tear welled up in her eye and she briskly wiped it away. "I like Colin — well, I did before now. I thought he was a really nice guy for my mom and now we find out that he's nothing but a bear-killer. So if that means he needs to get arrested or fined or whatever happens to poachers, then he deserves it."

Ontario Provincial Police
Crime Stoppers Division
Record of Citizen's Report/Complaint

Date: Saturday, September 29
Recording Officer: Constable Nichols
Name of individual: Anonymous
Address: Withheld
Phone Number: Withheld

Details of Citizen's Report/Complaint:

A phone call was made at 12:35 p.m. by a young male. A recording was made and filed #32683.

The male reported concerns regarding a farmhouse owned by Colin Braemarie, 1735 Brackenberry Road. On this property there is an alleged barn containing live bears as well as body parts of bears kept in a freezer. The speaker claimed to have overheard a conversation indicating that a deal would be executed next Saturday, October 6, involving the illegal selling of bears and bear parts.

Follow-up:

The recording and a copy of this report will be forwarded to Detective Ed Martin, who is currently leading an investigation involving poaching.

In case you're wondering, Dad, Constable Coleman gave me that copy of the police report. He felt sorry for me because of you making me write this, and he wanted to help. I would have liked to have seen your face when you received that report, now that I know it was given to you. Did you realize that it was Roy on the phone? I'm sure you did. You must have had a fit! I guess that explains all the extra jobs you gave us at home that week — you wanted to keep us busy and away from the farmhouse.

As for us, once we made that call, we figured that Mr. Braemarie would soon be arrested. Every day we expected the police to show up at Mr. Braemarie's doorstep with handcuffs, but nothing happened. As far as we could tell, it was business as usual at the farmhouse. I began to wonder if our call had been taken seriously.

By Wednesday, Roy and I had given up on the idea of a police raid anytime soon. We got our chores done quickly, as soon as we got off the school bus, and pedalled over to the farmhouse to meet Mindi, who was there with her mom, as usual. Roy had a little lesson on Ginger. He was terrible, shrieking like a girl whenever the horse started to trot. Mindi told him he'd catch on, but I think she was just being nice. I hadn't laughed that hard since Roy's shorts fell down to his ankles at the public pool in Mississauga, when he was showing off to a bunch of girls. He really is a schmuck!

By Friday, we were at our wit's end. The thugs were due back at dawn the next morning. If the police actually planned to respond to our call, it would be the last day of Mr. Braemarie's life masquerading as a law-abiding citizen. And the way Mindi figured it, that also meant he'd no longer be her mom's boyfriend, so it would also be the end of her spending time with his horses. It wasn't just his lifestyle that would be changed dramatically; we all had a lot to lose here.

We were supposed to go over to Cori's house that night for a sleepover. Can you imagine? Cori invited me along with Stacey and Mindi. She said that her dad insisted that she include me because I seemed like such a nice girl when he met me with Mindi in his office. I wasn't really looking forward to a whole evening with Cori, but I agreed to go for Mindi and Stacey's sake. However, at the last minute, Mindi bailed. She just really wanted to spend time with her beloved horses at the farmhouse, in case it turned out to be her last chance to be with them.

So that's how it came about that Roy and I ended up at Mr. Braemarie's farm that day after school. To share with Mindi her last visit with her beloved horses. We were the only two people who knew what was going on and who understood how she felt. Who would have known what was in store for us? And who knows how things might have turned out if we weren't there?

UNEXPECTED VISITORS

DATE: FRIDAY, OCTOBER 5

LOCATION: THE FARMHOUSE

As Roy and I cycled to the farmhouse, thunder rumbled in the distance. Dark clouds scurried across an ominous sky. I shivered as a huge gust of wind whipped my jacket around me. I bent forward and pedalled faster against its force.

"Why are we doing this again?" yelled Roy over the gale.

"It's Mindi's last visit with the horses," I gasped, trying hard to convince myself that this was a good idea.

We finally arrived. After we dropped our bikes on the side of the driveway, Roy turned to me. His face was serious.

"So, Sarah, like I said, we're staying far away from the barn. You and Mindi have your little visit with the horses and then we're out of here. Clear?"

I straightened my shoulders and gave him a mock

salute. "Yes, sir," I said. From the porch, I heard Mindi giggle.

"Quit joking around, Sarah," scolded Roy. "I'm trying to keep us out of trouble here."

"Oh, lighten up," I replied with a wave of my hand. "I was just kidding around. We have no intention of going anywhere near the barn."

We headed for the stable. Inside, we found Mr. Braemarie in the process of saddling up Candy, whistling while he worked. Ginger stood in her stall, all tacked up.

"Hello ladies," he turned to us with a smile. "And gentleman," he added, when he saw Roy.

We greeted him politely. It was hard to be nice to him when we knew what he was doing to those innocent bears.

"Wow, Colin, you have the horses ready for us," said Mindi, raising her eyebrows.

"Thought you could use a hand getting out there before the weather really hits. We're going to get a doozy of a storm — the phone line's already been knocked out with the wind," he explained. "I wanted to help out," he added with a shrug.

"Thanks," she mumbled nonchalantly.

Mr. Braemarie swallowed, then turned to Roy. "Are you planning to do some riding today?" he asked.

Roy reddened slightly. "No, I'm not much of a rider. Thanks anyway. I'll just watch Mindi and Sarah."

"I'll just have to give you a lesson myself one of these days." He grinned at Roy before turning back to us. "Why don't you girls get your helmets on now and get out there before the rain —"

The sound of an approaching vehicle stopped Mr. Braemarie cold. He cocked his head, listening. The sound grew louder and then stopped. Mr. Braemarie frowned, then hurried over to the door and looked out. I peeked around him. The black car was in the driveway in front of the barn.

"You'll have to excuse me, kids," he said, the frown deepening on his face. "It looks like I have some unexpected visitors." He turned to Mindi. A sheen of perspiration glistened on his forehead. "Maybe you'd better postpone your ride to another day. I … uh … don't want to be tied up with business, you know … in case you need my help or anything."

"We'll be okay, Colin. You don't need to help us," Mindi said. She didn't look at him. I knew that since she found out about the contents of the forbidden barn, she was having a difficult time being her usual friendly self with Mr. Braemarie. He looked at her, then looked over at the barn, then back at her. We heard car doors slam in the distance. Mr. Braemarie looked alarmed.

"Mindi, please don't leave the stable while those men are here," he pleaded. "I shouldn't be tied up for too long." He was edging out of the doorway. "It'll be all right. Just stay in here until I get rid of these guys, okay?"

"Okay," she said, focusing on Candy's mane.

Mr. Braemarie jogged to the barn, calling out to his visitors as he ran. Three men in black trench coats stood beside the black car, watching his approach. The sky flashed and rumbled. Thunder kicked in his stall. I turned back to the others. Their faces were grim.

"It's those men again," I reported.

"Well, duh!" Roy threw up his hands. "That's it! We're so out of here. I knew this was a bad idea. C'mon, let's blow." We ignored him.

"Those men weren't supposed to come back until tomorrow morning," I said, perplexed.

"I know," said Mindi. "Something weird is going on. Did you see Colin's face? He wasn't expecting those men. He never would have let me invite you over if he knew they were coming."

"Maybe they just want to go over last-minute details for tomorrow," I suggested.

"I hope so."

"In that case, they'll be gone soon and Roy can stop having a fit over there," I added.

It was true, Roy's face had gone from white to red to purple. "I still say we leave, and we leave now. Mr. Braemarie can handle those men just fine without us hanging out in his stable," he said, heading for the door.

"Just a minute, Roy. Will you listen?" I protested. "We're not in any danger; we'll just stay here until the men leave, like Mr. Braemarie said. Besides, we can't leave Mindi here by herself."

That got to him. He looked at Mindi guiltily. "I meant we *all* leave," he stammered.

"Mindi's worried about Mr. Braemarie," I continued. "Aren't you, Mindi?"

"Yeah, a little, I guess. Something feels wrong," Mindi replied.

Roy scowled. He looked back and forth between Mindi and I. "We stay right here. Nobody moves."

"Right," I said. "Until the men leave, that is."

Mindi led Candy back to her stall.

I peeked out the door at the barn. Mr. Braemarie and the men were standing together. I wished I could hear what they were saying. Mindi joined me.

"They're just talking," I told her. "They're probably checking on things for tomorrow morning."

"Yeah, probably," nodded Mindi, biting her lower lip.

We kept watching. Suddenly, Cheng, the drill sergeant, stepped towards Mr. Braemarie and pushed him hard. Mr. Braemarie stumbled back from the unexpected shove but managed to keep himself from falling. I caught my breath. Mindi grabbed my arm and gave a little startled cry.

"What? What's the matter?" asked Roy, as he hurried over and peered out from behind the doorway with us.

Things happened very quickly. Cheng and Morchan advanced towards Mr. Braemarie, who took a step backwards and held up his hands, shaking his head. Then Gorely pulled out a gun and aimed it right at him while the other two men flanked his sides. Gorely gestured to the barn and waited while Mr. Braemarie fished around in his pockets for the key. He fumbled several times trying to fit it into the padlock. Then they pushed him inside, the door slamming hard behind them.

"Oh my God!" cried out Mindi, reeling back from the doorway. "They're going to kill him! They're going to kill him!"

HELP!

DATE: FRIDAY, OCTOBER 5 (CONTINUED)

LOCATION: THE FARMHOUSE

I'd like to be able to report that we handled this crisis calmly and effectively, like true, seasoned detectives. But, in truth, we sort of freaked. Roy began screeching something about how we had to get out of there. Mindi fell to the floor, whimpering and holding her face in her hands. As for me, I simply froze. I literally couldn't take my eyes away from the closed barn door; I didn't know what to do — my mind wouldn't work and I couldn't get my body to move.

Thankfully, I finally managed to pull myself together. Roy stopped screeching and sat down beside Mindi and put his arm around her until she stopped whimpering. He kept telling her that everything would be okay, but I could hear the alarm still in his voice.

"We've got to call the police," I said. "Something bad could happen here. We need to get help."

"Let's go," Roy nodded curtly. His face was white.

"We'll call from Mr. Braemarie's house."

We started to move. Roy helped Mindi up from the floor.

"Wait a minute." Mindi's voice stopped us mid-stride. "Colin said the phone lines are out — we can't phone."

"Great!" Roy started to lose it again.

"Calm down!" I ordered. "Is there a cell phone we can use?"

"Yes, but Colin always keeps it with him."

"Where's your mom?" I asked.

"She's not here today," moaned Mindi.

"We'll have to go get Dad," said Roy, decisively.

He peeked out the stable door, then motioned for us to follow him. We ran for the driveway, going around the house, so we'd be blocked from view if the men were to step outside the barn. I wondered what would happen if they saw us, then decided I didn't want to find out. I made my feet go as fast as they could. I was acutely aware of the cold wind whipping around me as I ran, making my open jacket balloon out behind me. The house had never seemed so far from the stable before.

Roy got to the bikes first. He picked his up and called for Mindi to jump on behind him. I climbed onto my bike, my breath ragged as I looked over at Roy. His eyes were bright and large, bulging out of his face. It took two frustrating attempts before I was able to get both feet on the pedals and start my bike heading towards the road. I felt like I was moving underwater.

Roy and Mindi made it halfway down the long dirt driveway when his bike hit a rock and wobbled dangerously. He struggled for a moment while Mindi held on tightly but then completely lost his balance. The bike fell over; Roy and Mindi sprawled onto the ground. Cursing, Roy helped Mindi to her feet. Her palms were bleeding.

"This is nuts," Roy spat, red-faced. "We're wasting time. We've got to get help fast. Who knows what's going on in that barn!"

I got off my bike.

"You go ahead and get help without us," I suggested to Roy. "You can ride a lot faster without doubling Mindi. We'll stay here."

Roy's eyes bulged out of his face even more. "Oh, no! We go together. I'm not leaving you two alone here. No way."

"Roy, don't be stupid. We're not going to go anywhere near the barn," I protested. "Quit arguing with me and get going. The bears and Mr. Braemarie need help in there. Go get Dad!"

"Sarah's right," agreed Mindi. "We need help here fast. You'd go a lot faster without us."

Roy was clearly at a loss. I thought he was going to cry. "I'm not leaving you two here alone," he wailed. "We're *all* leaving."

"Okay, Roy, calm down," I said. He looked at me, startled, like he wasn't used to me being the reasonable one. "Why don't you and Mindi go on the bikes and I'll start walking? Once you tell Dad what's going on and help is on its way, you can come back and double me home."

"But ..."

"Roy! I'll be away from here. What do you think — the bad guys are going to follow me down the road?"

"You'd better start walking home!"

I scowled at him. "What do you think, I'm an idiot? Why would I want to stay here?"

He picked up his bike. "Let's go, Mindi. Sarah, start walking. I want to turn around and *see* you on that road."

Mindi hopped on my bike and followed him down the driveway. A deafening crack of thunder announced their departure.

I jogged down the driveway after them, anxious to get to the road and off Mr. Braemarie's land, away from the goings-on in the barn. Roy and Mindi were specks in the distance by the time I slowed to a speed-walk on the roadside. Now that I was alone, I wasn't feeling all too brave. Walking down a deserted road while thugs were occupying the barn just a short distance behind me was more than a little unnerving.

"There's nothing to worry about," I scolded myself aloud. "They want bears, not kids." The first drop of rain landed on my cheek. "Great!" I spat. "What more could happen?"

I had been walking for a while when I heard the rumble of an approaching vehicle. My heart skipped a beat. I don't know why — people do drive along this road, either direction connects you to other roads that take you into town. So, how do I explain my reaction? Paranoia? Whatever the reason, at the sound of that vehicle, I dove into the bush and hid behind a tree.

A familiar-looking gray Jeep Cherokee flew past. I'd been in that vehicle recently; it was Mr. Stedman's! I couldn't believe my eyes. Was he finally coming to investigate our anonymous tip? As he passed, I saw Mindi's white face peering out the back window, her eyes wide and searching; for me, I'm sure. Roy was beside her. What were they doing in there with him? I flew out of my hiding place and ran back towards the farmhouse. As I stumbled up the driveway, holding my side, I saw that the Jeep had pulled up behind the black car. Had Mr. Stedman called the police? Were they on their way? A million questions were going through my head. I darted into the woods lining the driveway and worked my way closer to the barn, staying hidden among the trees just in case someone came out of the barn.

Mr. Stedman stepped out from the driver's seat and strode up to the barn door like a man with a purpose. He turned and gave what he must have meant as a reassuring wave to Roy and Mindi, who were still sitting in his Jeep. Then, he slowly opened the door and stepped inside. What did he think he was going to do in there all by himself? He definitely should have waited for reinforcements. Just when I was about to run over to the Jeep to ask Mindi and Roy what was going on, the door to the barn opened once again. Out stepped Mr. Stedman with both hands in the air, followed closely by a gun-wielding Gorely.

I rocked back on my heels. I knew Mr. Stedman shouldn't have gone in there alone! What was he thinking? Had he told the thugs that the police were coming? Were they coming? Gorely walked Mr. Stedman back to the Jeep, pushing him with the gun. Roy and Mindi must have been having a fit, helplessly watching those men come toward them. What did Gorely plan to do? Shoot Mr. Stedman right in front of them?

"Open the door," barked Gorely. Mr. Stedman did as he was told. "Back up! You kids, get outta there!" he yelled.

I gripped a branch of the tree in front of me and held on. What did he want with Roy and Mindi? What had they done with Mr. Braemarie? I watched helplessly as Roy and Mindi stepped out of the Jeep. Mindi clung onto Roy's arm; she looked terrified. I watched in horror as Gorely ordered Roy and Mindi into the barn, holding that gun steadily at Mr. Stedman's back.

"What do you want with us?" asked Roy, his voice strong in spite of the fear I knew he must be feeling. I couldn't help it; I felt proud of him.

"Just walk!" growled Gorely, giving Roy a shove with his free hand that would have sent him flying if Mindi hadn't been gripping his arm so tightly. As it was, it pulled Mindi forward and they both almost pitched headfirst into the dirt. Mindi shrieked in protest and alarm but they regained their balance and had no choice but to do as they were told.

With a last glance behind her, Mindi screamed, "Help!" and then disappeared from my sight as Gorely pushed her across the threshold into the forbidden barn.

"Leave her a—" I heard Roy yell before the barn door thumped closed, abruptly cutting off all sound.

I stood there, shocked, feeling very alone and helpless. I had to do something to save them! But what? Were the police on their way? What was going on in the barn? I was in agony, pacing from one tree to the next, wringing my hands together. Did I stay to help Roy and Mindi or did I go for help? If I stayed, what could I do?

Before I made up my mind, one of the men came out of the barn. The tall, skinny, hyper one with the pebbly face. Morchan. He whistled as he walked to the black car, oblivious to the rain, like he was there visiting an old friend, not kidnapping kids and murdering a bunch of bears. He pulled a large black bag out of the trunk and set it on the ground, hunkering down to zip it open. He took out a long, black rifle — it looked very much like the one we found in the little secret room that Roy said was a tranquilizer gun. I gulped. He stood up and hefted the rifle over his shoulder, slammed the trunk shut, and picked up the black bag with his free hand.

A grumble of thunder, accompanied almost immediately by a flash of sheet lightning, announced the arrival of another vehicle. A large transport truck turned into the driveway, its brakes emitting a piercing screech as it pulled to a stop alongside the Jeep and the black car. The truck was nondescript except for its colourful mud flaps bearing Yosemite Sam pointing his guns and saying "Back Off!" A large man in jeans and T-shirt jumped down from the driver's seat.

"Tipper!" greeted Morchan. "You're just in time. We're about ready to start loading up." They spoke briefly, then together, they headed into the barn.

They're picking up the bears right now, I realized with a start. My head started spinning with questions. Why had the plan changed? What were they going to do with Roy, Mindi, and Mr. Stedman? Was Mr. Braemarie still alive? I admit I was, all of a sudden, in full-blown panic mode. All

I knew was that if help wasn't on its way, it was up to me to get it. They had Roy and Mindi! I could never forgive myself if something happened to them.

I was vaguely aware that the rain had become a steady downpour. In fact, even under the cover of the trees, I was soaked. Lightning flashed every few minutes and the accompanying thunder was getting louder. I absently wondered how wise it was to be under all these trees during a thunderstorm. I had no phone, no bike, and I needed to get help — right now! I hurried towards the back of the barn, twigs and branches whipping and scratching me in my haste, then, with a quick look to make sure the coast was clear, I sprinted toward the stable. The horses were my only hope for speed. And speed was exactly what was needed.

I was dimly aware of the whistling wind, the flashing sky, and the rumbling thunder as I ran faster than I'd ever run in my entire life. Too bad I couldn't run like that during track and field meets, or I'd actually get some ribbons. I dashed into the stable and ran directly to Ginger's stall, making her startle and whinny nervously. I fumbled with the door latch and wondered when it became so hard to open. Ginger sensed my agitation and tossed her head restlessly. Finally, I led her outside, trying my best to calm her down by talking soothingly — at least as soothingly as I could talk in my panicked state. Back out in the rain, I stuck my foot in the stirrup and swung my leg over her back. Taking a deep breath, I tried to steady my backside on the saddle.

"I can do this," I said aloud. I leaned down and stroked Ginger's neck. "Please help me, girl. I need you now. Mindi needs you." Then I clicked my tongue and dug in my heels. "Let's go!"

To my surprise, Ginger responded immediately, and we trotted towards the house, right where I was steering her. I silently thanked Mindi for being such a good teacher. I realized that I'd be in full view from the barn on my way to the road, but I didn't have much choice. I crossed my fingers that everyone would stay inside long enough for me to get to the road. I cast the barn a nervous glance. So far, so good; the coast was clear.

I forced myself to breathe and think about all the things Mindi had taught me about riding. Then I squeezed my legs, dug in my heels, and guess what? Ginger picked up speed and cantered. I was so pleased with myself that I almost didn't look over and check the barn again. But I did, and to my alarm, the door opened. Morchan and Cheng stepped outside. Morchan was waving his arms about and pointing at the truck.

"Oh, no," I whimpered.

I pulled Ginger to the left and we plowed into the woods. "Please don't see me, please don't see me," I chanted, not daring to look back again. I ducked my head low against Ginger's neck, trying to avoid the slapping branches as Ginger trotted through the trees. Finally, we emerged onto the road.

We were free! We made it!

"Good, girl, Ginger!" I exclaimed.

Then I leaned forward, squeezed my legs into Ginger's body like Mindi taught me, and pushed my heels down into the stirrups. Ginger picked up speed. Big-time. I hadn't gone very fast on a horse up to then, but I ground my teeth and refused to pull her back as I struggled to stay in the saddle. Heavy drops of rain needled into my face and blurred my vision. I blinked the water out of my eyes and prayed I made it home to Dad — before it was too late.

The journey home was like a blur of various sensations. I remember squeezing the reins tightly; bouncing about on the saddle, struggling to stay on Ginger's back; blinking as the rain pelted my face; and splashing through puddles. More than once, Ginger's hooves slipped on the sleek, wet pavement, and at one point, a low crack of thunder startled her badly and just about sent me flying. I have to give Ginger credit, though, she turned when I wanted her to turn and she went as fast as I could handle.

All the same, my house never seemed so far away. You know the saying that just before you die you see your life flash before your eyes? Well, I was watching the big-screen 3-D IMAX edition for the eighth time just as Ginger hurtled down my driveway. I was never so happy to sit back and yell, "Whoa!" in my life. I pried my stiff, whitened fingers loose from their death grip on the reins and slid weakly off Ginger's back. We were both drenched, Ginger with sweat as much as rain. Her nostrils flared as she gulped in huge amounts of air. I wondered when she'd last worked so hard.

I hurriedly led Ginger into the garage, my whole body quivering like jelly. I murmured promises of apples and carrots as I closed the door, shutting her inside. Then I took the porch steps two at a time, splattering mud and water this way and that.

"Dad! Dad!" I yelled, bursting into the house. "Where are you?"

Dad appeared, looking quite irritated. "Sarah, what have I told you about …" he began.

Dad, you were about to start telling me off for yelling in the house, weren't you? Then with one look at your poor, sodden, muddy daughter, your expression changed from irritation to shock and concern. You rushed right over to see if I was hurt. Thanks for caring, Dad. It was nice while it lasted, because it only took a moment for you to start yelling at me after all when you heard what I had to say…

"Roy and Mindi are in trouble," I blurted. "They're at Mr. Braemarie's barn …"

"I told you not to go there!" Dad shouted.

"… and these men took them inside. They have guns! They might have killed Mr. Braemarie!" I gasped.

"Roy and Mindi are …? Colin …?" he stuttered in disbelief.

I nodded, wondering how he knew Mr. Braemarie's first name. Then his expression hardened.

"When did this happen? How many men are there?" he asked, grabbing my shoulders, either to steady me or to hurt me. Who knows, he was pretty mad.

"I don't know, maybe twenty minutes ago," I moaned. "Roy and Mindi were coming here to get you, but then they went back to the barn in Mr. Stedman's Jeep, and then Gorely had a gun on Mr. Stedman and he made Roy and Mindi go inside, then Morchan got a big rifle out of the car that I hope was a tranquilizer gun, and then a big truck came … and Cheng was already inside … so …" I was rambling but I couldn't seem to help it.

"So five men. How do you ...?" His gaping mouth snapped shut. "Never mind. I need to get over there. I'll use the radio in the car." He ran up the stairs to his office, leaving me shivering in the hallway. In record time, he was bounding down the steps two at a time while strapping on his shoulder holster.

"You are going to stay here!" he yelled at me, holding a finger right up to my face. "Call your mother on her cell and tell her to get back here and keep an eye on you. Do not leave this house." The look he shot me with that last remark could have cut glass. I flinched. Literally.

He reached the door, then stopped and turned, his eyes boring into mine, his voice now controlled and steady. "You have a lot of explaining to do when this is taken care of, young lady." He ran out into the rain.

Then I remembered Ginger.

"Oh, oh," I said, running after him. "Dad!"

I was too late.

"*Sarah! There's a horse in my garage!*"

Dad was standing at the open garage door, already dripping, looking ready to kill someone.

"Sorry, Dad, that's how I got here."

I moved fast, leading Ginger out of the garage while Dad jumped into his unmarked police car. He immediately used the radio to call into the station. Of course, I was standing right there with Ginger, so was able to catch Dad's side of the conversation.

"It's going down *now*," he said. "Colin's in trouble. We were expecting these jokers tomorrow morning ... It's going badly. There're two kids in the barn against their will, one of them is Roy ... and Stedman from the

MNR … I have no idea … I'm heading over immediately … Yes, I'll meet the team there. Proceed with *extreme* caution."

Then the engine roared and Dad was moving, tires splashing down the driveway.

I stared after him, frozen to the spot.

"Colin's in trouble? *We* were expecting these jokers tomorrow?" I repeated dumbly. Understanding dawned. I'm thick, but I'm not entirely stupid. "Colin's in on it," I told Ginger. "He's one of the good guys." She bounced her head up and down as if in agreement. I suddenly felt a strong connection with Ginger, the horse who got me home safely, hopefully in time to save Roy, Mindi, and the bears. I threw my arms around her. "You're a good girl, Ginger. I just hope Dad isn't too late."

I led Ginger back into the garage. I started to unbuckle her girth, but I just couldn't make myself do it. I stared at it, willing my fingers to work the buckles, but they wouldn't. I couldn't imagine staying at home all alone while Mindi, Roy, and Mr. Braemarie were in mortal danger. I had to know what was going on. I had to help.

"We have to go back, Ginger," I said. She nudged my arm with her nose in response. I swallowed. Dad was going to kill me for this. Ah, heck, he was going to kill me anyway, what did I have to lose? Before I really knew what I was doing, I had my foot in the stirrup and I swung my aching leg back up over Ginger. I groaned and wondered if my muscles were up for more punishment. I turned Ginger towards the open garage door. My heart raced, keeping in time with my chattering teeth, but now that I'd made up my mind, I wanted to get back to that farmhouse more than anything else in the world. It didn't matter how much my body protested.

To the Rescue!

Date: Friday, October 5 (continued)

Location: The Farmhouse

I tried to kick-start Ginger into action, but she was reluctant to head back into the cold rain. I had to use all the tricks Mindi taught me to get her moving at all. I clucked my tongue, leaned forward, and dug in my heels over and over again, but only managed to get her to take a couple of steps. It seemed that as far as she was concerned, she'd already done her part and now only wanted to hang out and get some food. Part of me didn't blame her; I wouldn't have gone back out in that rain either if it wasn't a life or death situation.

"C'mon Ginger," I coaxed. "Let's go. Mindi needs us!"

Finally, she picked up the pace — a little — and we were out of the garage. Unfortunately, she headed for my house, not the road. I tugged on the left rein, trying to get her to turn. What was with her? I had to get back to that farmhouse and find out if Roy and Mindi were okay!

A bolt of lightning flashed overhead followed almost immediately by a deafening clap of thunder. Ginger startled and bolted suddenly towards the road, the way I'd been pulling on the rein. For one frightening moment, I was hanging on sideways, almost right off the saddle. With a grunt that was probably louder than the thunder we just heard, I hoisted myself back upright, finding the left stirrup again with difficulty. It's amazing what you can do when you're scared to death of falling off a horse!

Some heroic exit. But it didn't matter, Ginger was moving. We were cantering down the driveway. I got her turned onto the road and we were on our way to the farmhouse! I remembered what Mindi told me about how Ginger always travelled faster on the homeward trek, knowing that hay and water waited for her at the stable. I relaxed and figured the rest of the ride would be a breeze; she'd head straight for home.

Another flash of lightning and thunderous crack startled both of us — the storm seemed to be right overhead. Ginger reared and broke into a gallop. I think I screamed and tightened my grip, my heart pounding out of control. I know I wanted to get back to the farmhouse quickly, but this was craziness. We were ripping up the road like we were in the Kentucky Derby! I was being jostled about on the saddle so roughly that I could barely keep my feet in the stirrups. I leaned forward, pushed my heels down, and concentrated on staying on. The road looked blurry beneath our feet and made me dizzy. I forced myself to look up and not think about Ginger stumbling and falling on the wet, pot-holed road. I also tried not to think about how loudly she huffed with each stride, like she might be having a heart attack. Mindi wouldn't be too happy with me if I killed one of her beloved horses.

In no time, we were approaching the farmhouse. Up ahead, I saw my dad's unmarked vehicle parked on the road; he didn't appear to be inside. I had to get Ginger to slow down. She was puffing like a crazed beast. As for me, I wasn't sure if I'd be able to hold on much longer. Problem was, I didn't know how to get her to stop; I'd never gone that fast before. I tried to remember what Mindi told me to do if a horse bolts, but it isn't easy to think when you're on the back of a wild, raging monster trying with all your might not to fly off a wet, slippery saddle while being blinded by rain. And to think I once thought of Ginger as a calm, gentle horse!

"Whoa! Whoa!" I yelled in desperation. I don't even think she could hear me over the rain and ever frequent rumbles of thunder. "Stop! Stop!" I screamed even louder. It made no difference. What should I do? What should I do? Another rip of lightning lit up the sky almost directly above us, and the thunder boomed impossibly loud. Ohmigod! Were we going even faster now?

We flew past my dad's deserted car, my sopping hair streaming out behind me while the rain continued to fall, pelting my skin right through my jacket. We flew past Mr. Braemarie's driveway — I had to get this nag to stop! How did I ever think I had a connection with this out-of-control creature? She wasn't cooperating at all! Didn't she want to go home and eat hay? I kicked in my heels in frustration before realizing that was how to get her to go faster, not slower. Duh. I'm supposed to sit down! Believe it or not, it just occurred to me then. I forced myself to sit back; believe me, it wasn't as easy as it sounds. I was bouncing all over the place and terrified that I'd be flying off long before Ginger would be slowing down.

"Whoa girl!" I yelled as I desperately tried to sit down in the saddle. "Whoa! Stop!" I kept yelling and sitting, yelling and sitting, yelling and sitting until finally, whether it was because of anything I did or simply because Ginger was tiring out, we were actually slowing down. I don't really know or care why, the main thing was that we were finally at a manageable speed and I was still in one piece. That's all that mattered.

I turned Ginger around and we walked back towards the Braemarie farmhouse. I wanted to get there quickly but there was no way I was urging Ginger to pick up speed again. Lightning flashed overhead, and I clenched the reins tightly and spoke to Ginger in a soothing voice, trying to keep her calm when the thunder hit so that she wouldn't bolt again. As expected, she startled at the resulting boom but with much less enthusiasm than before and I was able to keep her under control. Maybe that connection was there after all.

"Good girl," I congratulated her, leaning down to pat her neck. "Let's get you back to the stable."

We stopped at the bottom of the Braemarie driveway and I peered down it, anxious to see what was going on. Nothing. No sign of anyone; the place looked deserted. Where was my dad? Why weren't the men all arrested and being taken away? I had to see what was going on, but first things first, I had to get Ginger back to the stable, and the last thing I needed was for my dad to see us. We clopped past the driveway and I steered Ginger into the bush where Roy and I first trespassed. We went slowly, following a twisting path of least resistance. As it was, I was constantly ducking out of the way of branches.

Then I saw my dad. He was standing in front of the house. He wasn't even in the barn yet! What was he waiting for? He was speaking into his radio headset and looking at his watch, his back to me. I turned Ginger a little farther to the right, staying as far away from him as possible. I kept watch as we passed and as a result received a good stinging slap in the face by a tree branch. Blinking back the tears, I silently urged Ginger forward.

We got safely past my dad and I took Ginger out into the open just in front of those prickly raspberry bushes. Once there, I swung my leg over and slid off her back, just about falling to the ground when I landed, my legs were so weak. I ignored them, threw the reins over Ginger's head, and tugged her towards the stable. We moved faster that way. Poor Ginger was used up. I knew how she felt. I led her into her stall, unbuckled her girth, and pulled off her saddle and pad. She was soaked underneath.

"Thanks for the crazy ride, girl," I mumbled. "Better than the midway."

She swung her head straight to her water bucket and I left her gulping noisily. I ran to the back of the stable and peered around. No sign of my dad or any other officers over at the barn. How could he just stand around doing nothing while Roy and Mindi were being held prisoners? Who knew what those men were doing to them! I'd be going nuts standing there waiting. Then I remembered what happened to Mr. Stedman when he didn't wait for backup and knew Dad was doing the right thing.

As for me, I didn't have to wait for anybody, and nothing was going to keep me from finding out what was going on in that barn. I made a dash straight through the open field. The ground was sopping. At one point, I lost my footing in a particularly large puddle and just about went down. Luckily, I managed to windmill my arms enough to save myself at the last minute. In any other circumstances, I would have been the first one to laugh at my klutziness, but as it was, I was in no laughing mood. I made it to the barn without being seen and kneeled down in front of our secret doorway, ignoring the puddles my knees formed in the mushy ground. I slowly pulled away the top board, leaned down, and peeked inside, hoping that my ragged breathing wouldn't echo, announcing my arrival to everyone inside.

The first person I saw through the bars of the cage in front of me was Mr. Braemarie. He was locked inside the food supply cage … along with Roy and Mindi. I breathed a sigh of relief: they were still alive! However, Mr. Braemarie looked like he'd seen better days. From my vantage point, his face looked a mottled purplish-blue colour and one of his eyes was closed and puffy. His chin was streaked red like he'd hastily wiped blood off it onto his red-smeared white T-shirt.

Roy and Mindi, in contrast, looked untouched. Scared and shocked but otherwise healthy. I sat back and thanked my lucky stars. I could never have lived with myself if either of them got hurt. Now where were the police? It was time to get them out of there before those thugs decided to get rough with them, like they had with Mr. Braemarie. As I watched, Mindi and Roy turned towards an approaching sound from the secret room we had discovered together.

"We've got all the stuff from the freezer," said Morchan, emerging from the corner of the barn carrying a box. He was followed by Cheng and Tipper, the transport truck driver. They were also carrying boxes. I pulled more boards away and stuck my head right through the opening in order to get a better view. Gorely and Mr. Stedman were also there, in front of the doorway leading to the small front room. Gorely was still holding a gun aimed at Mr. Stedman, who was kneeling on the floor over the open black bag that Morchan had retrieved from the black car earlier.

"Good," said Gorely. "We're about to start with the bears. You got the darts ready yet?" he asked Stedman, nudging him with his foot.

"Just about," said Stedman, frowning in concentration. "This is the last one." He was filling a cylinder the size of a finger with gleaming liquid. He wiped his forehead and pushed a stopper into the cylinder before setting it inside the black bag. "Done," he announced, pushing himself up from the floor with a grunt. "Twelve darts filled for eleven bears, with one extra, just like you asked."

I felt a pang of sympathy for him. I couldn't believe they were actually making Mr. Stedman, a Conservation

Officer, help them with this heinous crime! He must be dying to arrest them, not help. And I was sure he must feel horrible about Roy and Mindi getting locked up with Mr. Braemarie, especially since he was the one who brought them back to the barn with him. What had he been thinking, anyway? Did he honestly believe he'd just walk into the barn and stop a bunch of poachers single-handedly? Did he think he was some kind of superhero? I'm sure he was kicking himself now.

Gorely smiled. Not a pretty sight. "Leave the bag there and walk out to the truck," he said to Mr. Stedman, who moved to obey with a glance back at Mr. Braemarie, Mindi, and Roy.

"No!" cried Mindi. She grabbed the bars in front of her. "Let him come in here with us! He did what you wanted him to do, so leave him alone!"

"I'll be okay, Mindi. Don't worry about me," Mr. Stedman said.

Mindi's chin trembled while she watched Mr. Stedman being nudged out of the barn by Gorely's gun.

I was stunned. What was he planning to do to Mr. Stedman? Where were the police? I looked at Mindi, who was still gazing at the empty space where Mr. Stedman had been standing. I had to do something! Gorely might be hurting him. He needed help! I left my peephole and dashed towards the front of the barn, not sure exactly what I'd be able to do but wanting to be there anyway. I heard the barn door slam shut and peeked cautiously around the corner towards the driveway.

Mr. Stedman was still being prodded forward by Gorely's gun. My legs felt weak. What could I do if

Gorely planned to shoot him? Where was my dad? What was taking him so long?

"Get that gun off me!" said Mr. Stedman, suddenly turning and swiping the gun from Gorely's grasp. It rattled to the ground. My heart stopped; I couldn't believe my eyes. Mr. Stedman was going to fight back. Maybe he *was* a superhero! I held my breath and watched. Then Gorely laughed. Not his usual evil laugh but a real one. Like he was having fun. My eyebrows shot up to the sky. What was going on?

"Glad you're having a good time," complained Stedman, wiping his forehead. He jogged over to the back of the transport truck and yelled inside. "What's taking you guys so long? You've got to get started tranquilizing those bears. Do you think we have all night to get this done? Let's get on with it and get out of here!"

I felt like I'd been hit on the head with a club. I couldn't believe my ears. Mr. Stedman was talking to the thugs like he was one of them!

Morchan, Cheng, and Tipper jumped down from the truck. Morchan was scowling. "Look, Stedman, we're going as fast as we can. Relax."

"Relax?" Stedman laughed without humour. "You want me to relax?" He shoved Morchan up against the truck. "My daughter's friend is locked up in a cage along with some other kid. Braemarie saw my face, and you want me to relax? This is not the way this was supposed to go."

Gorely stepped up beside him and put a ring-studded hand on his shoulder. "Yes, we want you to relax. Don't blow this deal by getting all uptight. Don't worry about Braemarie, he has no idea you're working with us. I had a gun on you the whole time we were in the barn. As for the kids, you're the one who brought them here."

"I didn't know what else to do," Stedman sputtered, letting go of Morchan's shirt. "Mindi knows my car and she saw me on my way here. I couldn't just drive by her, I had to stop. And it's a good thing I did, Mindi and that boy were going to get the police."

Morchan shook his head and paced around Gorely and Stedman. "Sloppy. That's why I don't like working with amateurs."

Gorely scowled. "Why were those kids even around? You told me you took care of that."

"I did. Mindi was supposed to be at my house tonight, at a sleepover with my daughter, not here," protested Stedman. "And as soon as I got the copy of the Crime Stoppers tip, I let you know ..."

Gorely nodded impatiently, "Yeah, so we're here today instead of tomorrow. I know that. What I don't know is why we're stuck with two kids locked up in a cage. I don't like these extra complications, and I don't like you getting all uptight about it now when I need you to be calm and get the job done."

Stedman took a breath. "Okay, you're right. Let's get this done."

"That's better," said Gorely. "We don't want to blow this 'cause you can't keep your head on."

"I know, I know," muttered Stedman, running a hand through his hair. "Look, why don't you just tie me up or something? That way, when someone finally finds Braemarie and the kids, they'll never connect me to you."

Gorely glared at him and shook his head. "You're part of this whether you like it or not."

"Look, I'm the only one with connections here in Muskoka," insisted Stedman. "If I get caught, I'll never be able to set you up with a shooter or middleman again. Besides, I supplied the tranquilizer and prepared the darts, all that's left to do is point and shoot. Those bears will get nice and dopey in no time. Then all you'll have to do is lead them right into the cages in the truck. Simple. You don't need me anymore."

I shook my head, still unable to believe what I was hearing. Mr. Stedman, the man I went to for information, who said there were no poaching problems here in Muskoka, was working with the bad guys the whole time! He even tried to get Mindi and I out of the way by getting Cori to invite us over for a sleepover at his house! To make matters worse, the reason the poachers were here tonight instead of tomorrow morning was because of the Crime Stoppers call we made. I felt sick to my stomach. Why didn't we just tell Dad everything like we planned in the first place?

"He's right, Gorely," said Morchan. "We don't need him anymore. We just needed him to tell us how to deal with moving the live bears. He's done. He's just falling apart here. I say, tie him up." He spat at Stedman's feet and stalked away, heading back into the barn, followed by Cheng and Tipper, who also looked thoroughly disgusted by Stedman. Stedman looked hopefully at Gorely, totally oblivious to the wad of spit glistening on his hiking boot. Gorely shook his head again, frowning.

"Fine then," he said. "I'll tie you up. Don't worry, we'll take all the risk from here on in. You'll come off smelling like roses." Mr. Stedman's face lit up with relief. Gorely leaned in close to him, raising a finger to his face. "But if you ever breathe one word of who we are to anyone in authority, you'll be dead."

"I'd never say a thing," promised Mr. Stedman.

"Okay, so listen," said Gorely. "You're going to lay low for a couple of months after we're all done here, just like we planned. Do you remember the date and location of the drop-off for your payment?"

"Yes, I wrote it down. It's in my glovebox."

Gorely threw his hands up in the air. "You wrote it down?" He took a deep breath as if trying to regain control over himself. "For future reference, try to memorize little details like the pickup times and locations for payments. When you write something down, other people might end up reading it. Think." He tapped the side of Stedman's head to emphasize his point. He started to walk towards the barn, then turned back. "If you weren't so important, I'd pop you right now and get you out of the way for good." He pointed a finger at him and pretended to shoot, then resumed walking to the barn. Stedman paled.

I was seething now and hoped Stedman was good and scared. Serves him right for getting mixed up with these bear killers.

Gorely leaned into the open barn door and yelled, "Tipper! Get out here and tie up Stedman!"

Tipper stepped out of the barn. "Gladly," he said.

"I've got work to do inside," said Gorely. Then he headed back into the barn.

My heart lurched. They were going to start hurting the bears! Where on earth was my dad? I scurried back to my little doorway, anxious to see what was going on in the barn now. I felt numb. I couldn't believe that Stedman was part of this poaching ring the whole time. I fell down in front of the doorway and stuck my head back inside. I was shivering, my body was soaked right through. When were the police going to get here? What was taking so long? These thugs were going to have those bears drugged and loaded into the truck in no time. I couldn't just sit here and watch them do that.

I'd have to do something myself! But what?

Inside the Barn

Date: Friday, October 5 (continued)

Location: The Farmhouse

I squirmed my body through the little doorway and pulled my feet inside, twisting around to pull the boards up behind me. It looked like saving those bears was going to be up to me after all. So much for getting my dad's help. I wasn't sure yet what I could do, but I knew I had to do something.

I looked over at the cage where Roy, Mindi, and Mr. Braemarie were locked up. Mr. Braemarie was staring right at me! Startled, I jerked back, hitting my head on the rough barn board behind me. I stared back at him. Then he frowned and ever so slightly shook his head. I got his meaning. He was saying, Stay out of this, go away.

Fat chance.

Morchan stood in front of the cage beside Mr. Braemarie. He was pushing a dart into his rifle. Cheng stood in front of the cage across from Morchan, loading his own tranquilizer gun. Gorely stood by the door leading to the front room, his gun tucked into his belt, and looked at his watch.

"How long is this going to take?" he asked.

"Not long, boss," answered Morchan, raising his gun and pointing it towards the bear in front of him. "These darts have the maximum dosage in them."

Whomp!

Mindi screamed. I just about did too. As it was, I jumped enough to hit my head against that stupid barn board again. Roy put an arm around Mindi and spoke to her softly. Mr. Braemarie clenched the cage bars, alarmed.

"Got ya," said Morchan, lowering the tranquilizer gun. The dart poked into the bear's hide.

"That's too much!" yelled Mr. Braemarie, his knuckles white. "You're going to overdose her!"

Morchan turned to Mr. Braemarie. I could hear the evil grin in his voice. "Would you rather I killed it?"

"Stop!" yelled Mindi. "Leave the bears alone!" Roy looked alarmed and tried to shush her.

Morchan swung his gun towards her and pretended to shoot. "Bang, you're dead," he said. "So shut up."

"Don't talk to her like that!" growled Mr. Braemarie through the bars he clutched.

Quick as lightning, Morchan turned his weapon and slammed the butt against Mr. Braemarie's fingers. Mindi screamed. Mr. Braemarie pulled his hands back and gingerly held his damaged fingers.

"You shut up, too," said Morchan quietly, loading a fresh dart into the gun.

"Ignore them," growled Gorely to Morchan. "Get on with the bears." Cheng raised his tranquilizer gun and aimed at the bear in the opposite cage. I could see his face; he had a sparkle in his eye, like he was enjoying himself. I couldn't sit and watch another bear get shot. I stood up and took a step. Mr. Braemarie shook his head furiously at me, but I had to do something.

"Drop your weapons!" boomed a familiar voice. My dad and three other officers burst through the door, guns raised and aimed. Relief spread through me so intensely I thought I'd melt. I didn't know what I'd been about to do, but I was glad I didn't have to do it after all. I leaned heavily against the wall behind me.

Gorely spun around and pulled his gun out from his belt.

"I said drop your weapons," my dad yelled. "We have the barn surrounded."

"I don't believe this!" said Gorely, throwing his gun down in disgust. It hit the floor so hard that it sparked. Cheng dropped his tranquilizer gun. They both put their hands up. But not Morchan. He swung his gun around and aimed it directly at Roy, poking it through the bars of the supply cage.

"You drop *your* guns!" he yelled. "Or the kid gets enough tranquilizer shot into him to dope up a three- or four-hundred-pound bear. I wonder what it'll do to him."

My dad stared at Morchan, and his face darkened. Slowly, he lowered his gun.

"The rest of you too ..." yelled Morchan. The other officers slowly lowered their guns.

What were they doing? This wasn't supposed to happen! I was stunned as I watched the police officers lay their guns at their feet while Gorely and Cheng quickly retrieved their own weapons, raising them to cover the officers.

"Good work, Morchan," said Gorely. "Keep going with the bears. I'll take care of these guys."

"Not until I shoot this kid," said Morchan. "We've got that extra dart, and I'd like to see what happens to a scrawny kid when he gets all doped up. Should be kinda funny."

"Now, wait a minute," said Dad, alarmed. "You don't want to do that."

"Don't tell me what I don't want to do, old man," growled Morchan. "'Cause right now, I want to shoot this kid." He turned back to Roy, took aim ...

"*Drop your weapon, Morchan!*" It was me. I couldn't take it anymore. He was going to shoot Roy, and while normally he bugs the heck out of me, I still didn't want my only brother getting shot. Besides, I'd never be able to live with the attention he'd end up getting from my mom.

Everyone jumped at my voice. Everyone but Mr. Braemarie. He took advantage of the distraction I'd caused and knocked the tranquilizer gun out of Morchan's hands. It rattled to the floor inside the cage and he swooped it up and turned it on Morchan in one easy motion.

My dad caught on quickly. He jumped Gorely and wrestled the gun out of his grasp. The officer beside him knocked over Cheng and his tranquilizer gun rattled to the floor. The remaining two officers retrieved their own weapons from the floor and held them up, shouting for everyone to freeze and yelling that they were all under arrest. It was unbelievable how quickly a bad situation could change to good. All thanks to my big mouth.

As for Roy, as soon as he no longer had a gun aimed at him, he stumbled back against the old fridge, as if his legs had given out on him. Mindi rushed to his side. I wondered if he'd been scared enough to wet his pants and what Mindi would think of him then. Roy and Mindi huddled together and watched while handcuffs were slapped on all three men just before they were roughly escorted out of the barn.

I leaned against the bars in front of me as the reality of what I had just done sank in. My impulsiveness again. I had no plan. I just had to *do* something! It was a miracle it all turned out. It could have gone very differently. Then what? I guess I would have been watching the bears getting hauled away from the inside of a cage with Roy and Mindi, or worse …

"Get out from behind there, Sarah," my dad yelled, then he turned to Roy, Mindi, and Mr. Braemarie. "Are you all okay? Roy? Are you hurt?"

"We're all okay," said Mr. Braemarie. Mindi and Roy both nodded, Roy looking ashen.

I reluctantly made my way down the back of the cage to join them. I knew I was in trouble when I saw that Dad's face was an unhealthy scarlet colour, like the top of a thermometer that was ready to explode. I thought about escaping out the secret doorway and running far away until he'd cooled off. He watched me steadily as I walked towards him.

"I told you to stay home. Do you ever listen to me?" he said quietly. Too quietly, not a good sign.

"I know, Dad, but —" I started.

"*You know?* I told you to stay home," he repeated, his teeth clenched. Literally.

Oh boy.

"I'm sorry, Dad, I just wanted to help," I explained.

"You just wanted to help?" This was it. He was going to explode. "You'd help by doing as you're told!" He stared at me for a long moment, his mouth twitching. I think he was trying really hard not to blow, remembering that he had an audience and that he was on duty. Lucky for me. "We will be having a long talk about this at home," he said, at last. "Right now, I have a job to do."

He turned to Roy. "I'm going to make sure these guys get rounded up and off to the station safely, then I'll come back and get you out of there, okay?"

Roy leaned close to the bars. "But Dad, what about him?" he asked, tilting his head towards Mr. Braemarie.

"You're safe in there with Colin," said Dad. "I'll be right back." Then he left the barn, leaving them locked up in the stinky pig slop cage.

"Whoa," said Mindi. "I don't believe what just happened. It's a good thing you were here, Sarah."

"Don't tell her father that," said Mr. Braemarie, dryly.

"I'm glad you were here, too, Sarah. I don't care what Dad says, I could've been a goner," added Roy. He looked towards the doorway. "I wish I was out there watching those guys get taken away," he said wistfully, leaning through the cage bars.

"How do I get you out of there, Mr. Braemarie?" I asked, getting down to business.

"There's a little room back behind this cage ..." he began, turning and pointing towards the corner of the barn.

I waved him off. "I know where you mean," I interrupted, dashing off to the secret freezer room. Behind me, I heard him asking Mindi how I knew where I was going.

Inside the freezer room, I reached for the string that turned on the bare bulb and pulled it. The tranquilizer gun was gone. So were the bottles of liquid. The thugs took just about everything. I opened up the freezer. Yup. Empty. I rooted around the remaining items on the shelf but didn't see any keys. Finally, I spotted a ring of keys hanging on a hook behind the door. I grabbed them, ran back to the bigger room, and handed them to Mr. Braemarie. He took them gratefully. I knew how much those pig slop barrels stunk. Mr. Braemarie found the key he needed and worked it into the lock on the cage door, springing it open. Mindi burst out of the cage and threw her arms around me.

"Thanks for coming back for us!" she said, squeezing me in a tight bear hug.

Sorry about that bad pun, Dad, I couldn't help myself.

Now, you have to admit, it turned out to be a life-saving decision for me to go back into that barn after you told me to stay home. But even if I didn't distract the bad guys for you so you could save Roy's life, it was important for me to be there for my friend. It wasn't like you said, that I did everything I could to deliber-

ately disobey you. Sometimes, Dad, we have choices to make in life for other people.

And I also got them out of that stinky cage sooner than you were able to.

"You kids wait here," ordered Mr. Braemarie. He hurried over to the next cage where the tranquilized bear was lurching and stumbling about, making pathetic whining calls and banging off the cage bars. I felt sorry for the poor thing. Mr. Braemarie unlocked the cage door and slipped inside. Mindi gasped.

"Should he be going in there?" she whispered.

"Are you safe in there, Mr. Braemarie?" asked Roy.

"Don't worry," he answered. "This old girl's so dopey she doesn't know what's going on. She's only about eighty kilograms, and I heard Stedman say he was filling each dart with enough drug to take down the big males. I hope she's okay."

We watched as he gently reached down her furry back and pulled out the tranquilizer dart. She growled and swatted in the air, and even though there was little strength behind it, I was sure that those sharp claws would have done a lot of damage to Mr. Braemarie if they'd made contact.

"It's all right, girl," he crooned. "Take it easy." She whimpered and continued to swipe listlessly at the air in front of her. Mr. Braemarie carefully backed out of the cage, shutting the door behind him. "I don't think she'll be able to stay on her feet much longer." He looked down at the dart distastefully, shaking his head. "At least they didn't use a bullet on her. She's a zoo bear; she's never hurt a flea in her life. They weren't even going to lend her to us at first."

"So that's where you got the bears, the zoo?" I asked.

"Some of them," nodded Mr. Braemarie. "Others came from wildlife centres and sanctuaries. The rest were live-trapped from nuisance calls and brought here."

I noticed Roy and Mindi's puzzled looks. I smiled.

"Mr. Braemarie isn't a poacher like we thought he was," I explained. "He's working with Dad. This was a sting operation to catch poachers!"

Understanding dawned on Mindi's face. Mr. Braemarie laughed as she hugged him. "I was so worried that you were a poacher and that Mom and you would break up and that I'd never see Candy and Ginger again!"

"Glad to hear you just use me to get to my horses," he chuckled.

"No, I didn't mean it like that." Mindi blushed.

Mr. Braemarie hugged her again. "I'm glad you know I'm not a poacher, too. I wouldn't want you to think that I'd do something like that."

"Did you know that we were suspicious of you?" I asked.

"I wondered, especially since Mindi hasn't been her usual friendly self with me lately. Your father let me know right away when you asked to come here with Mindi. He thought it would be best to discourage you from visiting. He told me how nosy you can be, and apparently even he underestimated you."

"But you knew I was coming here with Mindi," I said, frowning.

He cleared his throat. "Yeah. Well, my attempt to keep you away by telling Mindi you weren't allowed over wasn't successful for very long. Turns out she can be a headstrong girl." He looked over at Mindi who blushed again. "Then, when I talked to your dad about it, we decided you'd get too suspicious with both of us not letting you visit. So I tried to scare you off instead."

"By threatening me in the stable?" I asked. "Telling me that I could get hurt by nosing around too much?"

"Yes. I wasn't too successful there, either," he said, solemnly.

"You just made me more suspicious of you," I agreed. "That's when I knew for sure that I had to get into this barn and see what you were keeping inside."

He shook his head. "Boy, your father wasn't kidding around when he said that you're one nosy kid." I looked at him, wondering if I should take that as a compliment or an insult.

I turned at the sound of voices coming from the front room.

"I can't tell you how sorry I am that I got Mindi and your son involved in all this, Detective Martin." It was Mr. Stedman speaking. I scowled. That two-faced, lying ...

Dad walked into the room, Mr. Stedman a step behind, rubbing his wrists as if they were tender. I was happy to see that they were red and sore looking. Tipper must have had him tied up nice and tight, just as I'd hoped.

Dad grunted. "It's not standard procedure to bring youths to a potential crime scene, but you'll have a chance to give a complete statement back at the station. You know how it goes. Colin Braemarie will join us. He's been working with us undercover to infiltrate this poaching ring," he explained.

Mr. Stedman's eyes widened. "He has?" He looked over at Mr. Braemarie as if noticing for the first time that he was no longer trapped in a cage. Then he saw me. "You! You're here, too!" he said, frowning. "You girls are supposed to be at my house with Cori." He stopped rubbing his wrists and let his hands dropped limply by his sides. His wrists! They were red but ...

"Dad! Why isn't he wearing handcuffs?" I asked, startled.

"Who?" he snapped, clearly not wanting to hear anything out of me.

"Mr. Stedman," I said. "He's working with the poachers."

"What are you talking about, Sarah? He's a Conservation Officer," he explained impatiently.

"Dad, I heard them talking out there. He was working with them, I'm telling you," I said.

"Just like Mr. Braemarie was working with them?" he asked, one eyebrow up. "For your information, I found Mr. Stedman tied up outside. You need to step down now and let me handle this. You've helped enough for one day." I got the look again, the one that could cut glass.

"Dad!" I protested. "I heard them talking outside. I'm telling the truth. He asked Gorely to tie him up so he'd look innocent when you found him."

Mr. Stedman had broken into a sweat, but his voice was clear and steady. "I don't know what she's talking about," he said. "She must have misunderstood. I had a gun on me the whole time, just ask Braemarie and the kids. They made me fill the darts with the tranquilizer and then they took me outside and tied me up to keep me out of the way."

Dad looked over at Mr. Braemarie, who shrugged. "He had a gun on him anytime I saw him."

Dad looked back at me, and his face hardened. "Sarah, when will you learn that you can't just go around making accusations with no evidence to back them up?" He turned back to Mr. Stedman. "I'm sorry about all this. It's the excitement. It's easy to misunderstand what's going on."

"I understand, Detective," said Mr. Stedman, wiping the sweat from his upper lip. "No harm done."

Then it occurred to me. Like I've always said, I may be slow but I'm not stupid.

"I have evidence!" I blurted.

"Sarah!" yelled Dad. "Stop this!"

"No, I do," I insisted. "It's in his Jeep. There's a note in Mr. Stedman's glove compartment saying when and where he's going to get paid for helping the poachers."

The room crackled with tension. Stedman tensed, ready to bolt. Mr. Braemarie moved to his side, ready to grab him if he did. But he didn't need to worry. Mr. Stedman realized he was caught. He sighed, his body sagged.

"She's right. I was involved," he said quietly. Mindi gasped, and her hands flew to her face. He looked at her sadly. "I don't know what came over me, to get involved with poachers. I've never done anything like this before." I have to admit, he did look sorry. Sorry he got caught, most likely.

"The money's good," answered Mr. Braemarie, grimly.

Dad put handcuffs on Stedman and walked him out to his waiting police car, explaining how he'd be giving his full confession at the police station, and if he knew what was good for him, he'd also tell them everything he knew about the poaching ring.

"I can't believe Mr. Stedman was part of all this," moaned Mindi, once they were out of the room. "Poor Cori! She's going to be devastated."

"I know," I agreed. "I couldn't believe it either, but I saw it with my own eyes."

"Okay, kids," said Mr. Braemarie, clapping his hands. "I'm going to arrange for the vet to get out here and take a look at this poor bear ..."

We all looked over at the tranquillized bear. She was now slumped on the floor of her cage, looking at us with bleary eyes.

"... then I guess we all better get ourselves to the station."

"Cool," said Roy with a grin.

Local Conservation Officer Arrested in Poaching Sting

Bracebridge, October 6

Harry Stedman, a local Ministry of Natural Resources Conservation Officer, along with four other men, was arrested at a farm outside the town of Bracebridge yesterday. Charges laid included poaching (the unlawful taking or killing of game), with the intention of selling bear parts in the international black market. These arrests were the result of a sting operation organized by the OPP in conjunction with the RCMP and Environment Canada Intelligence Officers.

Detective Ed Martin, OPP Bracebridge Detachment, led the investigative team. A mock bear farm was constructed at a local farmhouse outside of Bracebridge. This bear farm was presented to potential buyers as a bile gathering operation, similar to the bear farms that are being slowly eradicated in China. The bile gathered from bear gallbladders has unique medicinal qualities that are especially valued in traditional Chinese medicines, making the black market trade so lucrative.

While appearing remorseful, Harry Stedman refused to comment. It has been conjectured that Stedman's involvement in past Special Investigations Unit poaching investigations allowed him to make connections with various suppliers and traffickers of bear and other animal parts, thereby providing this opportunity for criminal involvement, allegedly his first time on the wrong side of the law. Bear galls range in prices on the foreign black market from $2,000 to $10,000, even as high as $50,000 in some parts of the world.

Colin Braemarie, an Environment Canada Intelligence Officer, was recruited to run this makeshift bear farm. He acted as the owner-operator, tended the bears, and made the connections with potential buyers. "I was fortunate to have phenomenal support from provincial zookeepers, who orchestrated the recruitment of the majority of the bears," said Braemarie. "They helped with the set-up of the barn and taught me everything I needed to know about the daily care needs of the bears. Also, the bears were monitored closely by a large animal vet to ensure that they weren't overstressed during their stay here. In addition, we used the barn as a temporary holding area for confiscated bear parts seized during previous searches and investigations. This added to our authenticity to the potential buyers.

"During their stay at the mock bear farm, the bears were treated humanely. No bears were hurt during the course of this investigation," assured Braemarie, "and now that the investigation has concluded, they will all be returned to their home environments — whether that was a zoo, a sanctuary, or the wild."

With Canada being the largest remaining habitat for black bears, illegal trade is increasing. A recent estimated worldwide value of the illicit trade in wild animals was more than $10 billion a year; higher than the black market for arms. With statistics like these, it is apparent that investigations such as this one will become more common.

Well, Dad, it looks like my report is finished, at last.

I want to say, once again, how incredibly sorry I am. I have to admit, you do have a point when you say that my involvement, or as you like to put it, interference, led to Mr. Braemarie, Mindi, and Roy being held against their will in the barn. But how was I to know that Mr. Stedman would tell the poachers about our Crime Stoppers call, making them change the date of the pickup? And how could I have known that those greedy poachers were going to double-cross Mr. Braemarie and decide to steal all the bears, not just the ones they agreed to buy? You didn't have any of that information either.

If you really think about it, it was a good thing I was at the farmhouse that day or the whole sting could have been blown. Those poor bears would never have been returned to their homes, and who knows what would have happened to Mr. Braemarie? I'm not even going to mention that, if it wasn't for me, you would have had no idea that Mr. Stedman was a bad guy! You would have let him loose to strike again!

And let's not forget, as I've outlined very clearly throughout my report, you *played a very large role in influencing many of my "bad" decisions:*

First of all, stopping me from visiting a new friend — really, Dad! Don't you watch Dr. Phil*? That only made me want to visit her more!*

Secondly, you could have been more honest with me about Mr. Braemarie's farm. I'm not really so young and foolish that you have to protect me all the time. I know you couldn't tell me everything — but enough to prevent me from investigating on my own would have made sense, wouldn't it?

Finally, imagine a father letting another man threaten his own daughter — even if it was just to scare me away. I'm shocked! But Mr. Braemarie's threatening words only increased my suspicious and curious nature — and you should have known that they would. (By the way, Mr. Braemarie bought me my own riding helmet since he felt so bad about the way he spoke to me in the stable, so it actually worked out well for me in the end.)

I guess you're just going to have to face it, Dad. I'm a curious kid, and if you want me to stay out of your way during these kinds of investigations, you're just going to have to do a little more sharing, don't you think?

So Dad, what else can I say? Oh, I know:

- *I've really learned from my mistakes this time.*
- *I'll try to remember that all choices have consequences, just like Roy says you keep telling me.*
- *I'll mind my own business.*
- *I'll live my life the way you want me to live.*
- *I'll stop thinking for myself.*
- *I'll blindly obey you at all times no matter how silly your rules are.*

Are you buying any of this, Dad? Do I need to keep making stuff up that you want to hear?

You gave me this assignment so that I had to follow through like a real detective who would write a report outlining findings and conclusions. You wanted to introduce me to the more dreary part of the world of investigation. At first, I thought it was going to be awful, just like you hoped, but once I started, other than the solitary confinement, I didn't mind writing this report at all. Actually, I kind of liked it! In fact, I think I'll start keeping a journal.

So, I guess your plan backfired. Sorry about that (not really).

I still really want to be a detective, like you, Dad.

Love,
Sarah

Dear Sarah,

I just finished reading your report, and since you put so much time and effort into writing it, I thought it was only fitting to reply to it in writing. I think I now know more about you than I ever cared to know. You weren't kidding when you said you were going to tell me everything. I expected about a dozen pages. It took almost a week to get through the whole thing! Well, a couple of times I had to stop reading because I was losing my temper. But like you said, this *was* your punishment, so I managed to stop myself from stomping up to your room and yelling at you all over again.

I still have a couple of concerns. One is that you continue to think you were instrumental in Stedman's capture and arrest. How many times do I need to tell you that we would have figured it out without you? Sure, we got him a little faster with your help, but we would have gotten there regardless. Morchan was ready to talk faster than your Mom's new pig eats its slop. We would have gotten it out of him in no time.

My other concern is that you still want to be a detective. It's a very dangerous job, Sarah. Can't you get interested in something else? What about being a teacher? Or a veterinarian? They're much safer professions. Believe me. Why would you want to deal with the criminals of this world? It just turns you into an old grump like me. You said so yourself, how you don't want to be around me when I'm angry.

I was really hoping to dissuade you from detective work with this assignment, but I can see that I haven't. In fact, it's very clear to me that I'll have to keep a very sharp eye on you from now on.

I'm on to you.

Love,
Dad

My New Journal

Date: October 24

This is my first entry in my new hard-covered journal. I plan to record the events of my life. Like Dad says, trouble likes to follow me around. I might as well start writing about it. Who knows, I may have to defend my actions again someday, so this time, I'll be ready.

Since the arrest of Mr. Stedman, Cori hasn't spoken a word to me or Mindi. First of all, she wasn't at school for over a week. Now she turns her back when I walk into the room, and she refuses to work with me if the teacher asks her to. She had to serve detention the other day because she wouldn't sit in the same group as me during science class. She hates my guts. I can see it in her eyes. I guess I can live with that. I'd probably hate me too.

As for Mr. Stedman, he avoided a jail term by giving the police all his contacts within the poaching ring. As a result, more people were arrested. Mr. Stedman ended up being slapped with a — in my opinion — petty fine for his role in the bear poaching ring, but much worse, he lost his job with the Ministry of Natural Resources. He walks around town, fulfilling his community service hours, hunched over, defeated. I almost feel sorry for him. He probably hates my guts too. Oh well.

Mr. Braemarie and Ms. Roberts are still seeing each other. Turns out, Ms. Roberts knew all along that Mr. Braemarie was working with the police, but she didn't know the minor details, like he was keeping bears in his barn. Might have been nice for her to tell Mindi what she knew, don't you think? Speaking of Mindi, she still gets to spend lots of time at the farmhouse with her beloved horses so she's happy. The difference is that now I'm actually allowed to go over there too. No more lying! Unfortunately, Roy often likes to tag along with me so that he can make goo-goo eyes at Mindi while we're riding. I don't know how she can stand it. Funny enough, Mom and Dad have also been spending some time at the farmhouse. Mr. Braemarie's a big fan of barbecues and get-togethers. I'm sure glad he didn't turn out to be a bad guy after all.

Well, that's all I have to say for now, but I'll be writing in you again, real soon!

S.

Acknowledgements

I wish to thank my good friends and critique group members, Lizann Flatt and Wendy Hogarth, for their invaluable feedback and suggestions in the writing of this story. I always appreciate their unwavering support and optimism. Also, thank you to Natasha Pattison, whose expertise about horses proved quite helpful.